HAMMER OF TH

Also by Leo Kessler in the *Wotan* series

SS PANZER BATTALION
DEATH'S HEAD
CLAWS OF STEEL
GUNS AT CASSINO
THE DEVIL'S SHIELD

Leo Kessler

Hammer of the Gods

Futura Publications Limited

A Futura Book

First published in Great Britain in 1975
by Futura Publications Limited

ISBN 0 8600 72045

Printed in Great Britain by
Cox & Wyman Ltd,
London, Reading and Fakenham

Futura Publications Limited
49 Poland Street, London W1A 2LC

'This battle is to decide whether we shall live or die. The battle must be fought with brutality and all resistance must be broken – *in a wave of terror!*'

Adolf Hitler to Colonel von Dodenburg,
SS Battle Group Wotan, 10th December, 1944.

ONE: THE LAST OFFENSIVE

'The Meuse with one tank, von Dodenburg – that's all I ask of you!'

SS General Kraemer to Colonel von Dodenburg

I

Soon it would be dawn. The hard silver stars were beginning to disappear and a cold wind which heralded the new day had commenced sighing softly through the snow-heavy firs of the Ardennes forest. On the horizon, which was Germany, the soundless flickering of the heavy guns was the only indication that this was a combat zone.

Dug in on either side of the little Belgian border road, the green GIs of the U.S. 99th Division stamped their frozen feet and shivered underneath the olive-drab blankets they had wrapped around their helmets. Time and again they looked at the faint green gleam of their watches and wished their spell of duty were over so that they could stumble through the deep snow back to the blue fug of the guard hut, with its red-roaring pot-belly stove.

After only nine days in the line on the Ardennes ghost front, where there had been no fighting now since September, the young soldiers knew it wasn't the Heinies they had to be scared of, but the punishingly cruel winter conditions. Already a couple of hundred men of the Division had been hospitalized with frostbite and according to the canteen commandos back at Divisional HQ at Butgenback, there was worse to come in December with temperatures falling way below zero.

PFC Horatio Hardy Smith, crouched shivering over the little section's .5 machine-gun, tugged out a D bar from beneath his tightly buttoned overcoat (he had already learned to call the hard chocolate the 'Führer's secret weapon' like the veterans did) and had just begun to peel off the wrapping with clumsy frozen fingers when he heard a faint, but definite, rusty rattle. He started violently and dropped the choclate bar into the snow.

'Joe,' he called in an urgent whisper to the next foxhole, '*Joe Rizzio!*'

'What the hell d'ya want?' Corporal Rizzio responded grumpily.

'Did you hear that?'

'Hear what?' Rizzio asked, shivering violently beneath his blanket, his eyes tightly screwed together as if he could blot out the miserable cold that way.

'A tank – there's a tank out there somewheres!'

'Aw, go and crap in ya hat,' Corporal Rizzio said scornfully. 'There ain't no gaddam tanks in this area within—'

He stopped, suddenly wide-awake. Thrusting his blanket to one side, he cocked his head so that he could hear better, staring in sudden fear into the gloom. 'Christ on a crutch!' he cursed. 'You're right, Smith – there *is* a tank out there.' He swallowed hard and then snapped: 'Okay, guys, everybody stand to! And make it goddam snappy!'

There was a fevered fumbling with weapons, as the scared GIs flung off their blankets, grabbed their MI rifles, clicked the safety catches up and hastily spread their grenades on the lips of their foxholes.

PFC Horatio Hardy Smith hardly dared breathe. His hands, grasping the icy butt of the machine-gun, were wet with sweat. The sound was getting louder and it was definitely a tank. He swallowed hard and tried to control himself. He had heard tales about how the Kraut tanks would spin round and round over a foxhole until the earth gave way under the tracks and the whole weight of the metal monster descended upon the terrified GI below and crushed him to pulp.

'I don't think it's coming from the direction of Krautland, Corp,' a youthful voice said out of the gloom. 'Seems to be behind us.'

'Yeah,' Rizzio agreed with a sudden sigh of relief. 'Buellingen way by the sound of it.' He raised his head above the lip of the foxhole, his carbine still held at the ready.

The unmistakable high shape of a Sherman tank, a black shadow against the white of the snow, had turned the bend and was advancing up the little road, the thin blue beams of its blacked-out headlight illuminating the spiked outlines of the snow-bound firs.

'It's one of ours,' said Rizzio. 'A Sherman'.

PFC Horatio Hardy Smith whispered a sudden prayer of thanks, the vision of his mangled body crushed at the bottom of a blood-filled foxhole rapidly disappearing from his mind's eye. 'Shall we stand down, Joe?' he called happily.

Rizzio did not answer for a moment. He was staring apprehensively at the strange tank advancing so purposefully on them. It was buttoned down completely. No one was on the turret and there was something uncanny about its slow yet determined progress. To Rizzio, once a keen science fiction movie fan, the Sherman's headlights made it look like some fearsome blue-eyed monster, feeling its way through the primeval forest in search of its human prey.

'The sarge didn't say nuthin about no tanks when we came on guard,' he said hesitantly. 'Did he?'

'Oh hell, Corp,' someone answered carelessly. 'You know the sarge, he don't know his goddam ass from—'

The speaker never finished his sentence. There was a sudden soft crack. A hush as a flare burst right in front of the sentries, bathing them in its unreal, blood-red light.

'*What the goddam hell's going on?*' yelled Rizzio.

His answer was another flare. And another. They came from all sides, turning night into day, blinding the GIs with their brilliant reds, whites, greens. Rizzio spun round, his arm held up in front of his eyes against the glare. He could see nothing. The hissing lights blinded him. But he could hear the rumble of the tank tracks getting louder and suddenly his nerve broke.

'*Krauts!*' he screamed, and sprang out of his foxhole.

'Run for it, guys!' PFC Horatio Hardy Smith yelled in fear, kicking over his machine-gun as he clambered out after the corporal, now pelting across the glowing, blood-red snow, his carbine already flung away in panic.

'*KRAUTS – RUN FOR IT!*' the frightened cry was taken up everywhere.

As if to lend speed to the GIs mad flight, the strange Sherman's turret machine-gun opened up with a high-powered scream. An angry red-and-white morse of glowing tracer bullets cut the air. Lead stitched a crazy pattern in the snow at their heels. Yelling hysterically, the GIs flung themselves into the firs, the bullets striking the branches like heavy summer rain. In their panic they blundered deeper and deeper into the forest, pursued by the death-dealing bullets.

2

'All right, William Tell – that's enough of that!' In order to emphasize his command, the red-faced Sherman commander aimed a vicious kick at the gunner's leather-helmeted head, as he pushed up the turret cover. 'They've creamed their knickers already – and we wouldn't like a nice bunch of lads like that from the land of unlimited possibilities to get themselves seriously hurt, would we now?'

The young gunner mumbled something under his breath.

'And your mother too!' the Sherman commander said without rancour, his eyes already searching the abandoned American position. But the Amis had fled. Satisfied, he pressed his throat mike. 'All right, driver,' he ordered, 'rein in yer chariot, will yer, so that we can pick up our two Belgian asparagus Tarzans.'

The driver braked the 30-ton tank to a stop. Cupping his ham-like red hands around his mouth, the big commander yelled. 'Harry – *Hairless Harry.* Get yer arse over here – quick!'

Hairless Harry, the Belgian front-runner[1] and his pal Starving Sepp, who had blinded the Americans with the flares doubled towards the waiting tank through the glare of the dying flares. A second later the driver had rammed home first gear. A thick cloud of blue smoke swept over the abandoned American position. With a rumble of rusting tracks, the strange tank set off again towards the frontier and Germany.

* * *

Outside in the muddy Eifel farmyard, the dispatch riders came and went, slithering wildly through the thick mud. A panzer grenadier was urinating against the bullet-pocked wall. A little

[1] Term used for an undercover agent who crossed the lines in World War II (*Transl.*)

further on, the goulash cannons were boiling merrily, preparing the breakfast soup and the thin *ersatz* nigger sweat. It was nearly eight o'clock at the headquarters of SS Battle Group Wotan.

'Well,' asked Colonel Kuno von Dodenburg, Wotan's CO, 'did you pull it off?' He looked across his paper-littered desk at the strange trio.

Senior Sergeant Schulze, his massive frame flanked by two ragged Belgian renegades, raised his right leg slightly and gave a contemptuous fart. 'Easy as peeing in a pot, sir. We was in the Ami depot, had pinched their Sherman and was on our way – all within twenty minutes.' He jerked a dirty, big thumb behind him, 'Those Amis up there in the hills are real greenbeaks, sir, with the eggshell still behind their spoons.'

Colonel von Dodenburg turned to the two Belgians who had thrown in their lot with the Germans when the German Army had been forced to evacuate their country the previous September. 'I'd like to thank you for your effort. I'll see it is noted in the proper quarters.'

Hairless Harry, a morose doleful man from the canton of St Vith who was completely devoid of hair (even his eyebrows had gone) muttered something unintelligible. Starving Sepp, his constant companion, an emaciated Belgian who was always eating, swallowed the hunk of bread he had been chewing surreptitously, and gasped: 'We try to do our best, Excellency.'

Schulze looked down at him scornfully. '*Excellency!*' he sneered. 'Great crap on the Christmas tree – what do you think this is? The Belgie Army, with finger bowls and wearing frilly lace knickers? No, this is the SS, my lad. Excellency, by Christ!'

Von Dodenburg held up his hand to silence the big Hamburg ex-docker, who had fought at his side on every battle front in Europe since Wotan had been formed five long years before. 'All right, Schulze, that's enough of that. You two can go and get yourself some breakfast down below if you want.'

'A request,' said Starving Sepp, looking up at the red-faced German NCO cheekily, 'your Excellency.'

'Yes?'

'Could his Excellency see his way to instructing the gentlemen of the goulash cannons to give us poor foreigners an extra helping of their fine soup?' He smiled winningly at von Dodenburg, displaying a mouthful of big yellow horseteeth. 'And perhaps a second cup of that excellent nigger sweat?'

The handsome young SS Colonel smiled. 'All right, tell the kitchen bulls they are to give you as much soup and coffee as your skinny guts will stand. Is that all right?'

The skinny Belgian threw him a happy parody of a military salute and hastily pushed his dour companion to the door.

'Well, I'll shit in the wind,' Schulze exclaimed as the two of them clattered down the stone stairs that led to the courtyard and the kitchen. 'That little Belgie would flog his own mother for a sausage sandwich or a tin of Old Man! And now I've a question sir,' he said, staring down at his CO. 'What was it all in aid of, sir – I mean nabbing the Ami tank and everything?'

Von Dodenburg shrugged helplessly. 'I don't really know, Schulze. The order to steal the damned thing came from HQ Sixth SS Panzer Army – from the Butcher Boy personally'[1]

Schulze whistled softly through a gap in his front teeth. 'The Butcher Boy, himself, eh!'

'Frankly, why an Army Commander concerns himself with such things is beyond me.' Von Dodenburg hesitated. 'Though I can guess, Schulze,' he added.

'Guess what, sir?'

'Well, I thought after the terrible beating and losses the Wotan took in the Battle of Aachen[2] we had been sent to this God-forsaken Eifel for a rest. But these papers seem to indicate that the – er – Führer's Fire Brigade, as those elegant gentlemen at Army HQ are pleased to call us, is meant for something less pleasant.' He rapped his knuckles on the sheaf of papers lying before him on the farm-kitchen table which now served him as a desk.

Schulze tugged the end of his nose. 'What do you mean exactly, sir?'

[1] General Sepp Dietrich, commander of the 6th SS Panzer Army, who reputedly had once been a butcher boy (*Transl.*)

[2] See *The Devil's Shield* for further details. (*Transl.*)

Before von Dodenburg could answer, a harsh NCO's voice down below in the courtyard bellowed: *'Turn out the guard – at the shitty double, will yer!'* Hobnailed boots scampered over the hard-pressed snow. *'Get in line there – come on, move those big base stallion-arses, will yer!'*

The two men in the office could hear the harsh stamp of marching boots and the crisp sudden burst of the new arrivals' song, rapped out by two hundred or more young enthusiastic throats. Hastily von Dodenburg rose to his feet and strode to the window. Schulze followed him and peered over his shoulder at what was happening below.

Wreathed in their own grey breath, their unlined youthful cheeks glowing with good health, the new arrivals from the depot crunched over the snow in perfect formation and stamped confidently past the shabby line of veterans who made up the little guard.

'More cannon fodder?' Schulze queried softly.

Von Dodenburg turned away from the little farmhouse window, traced with the bitter lines of the frost, and shook his head slowly. 'Not cannon fodder, Schulze. Volunteers, every man of them. And not only Germans. Down there, there are Danes, Swedes, Norwegians, Dutch, Belgians – even a handful of English – men from all over Europe, eager to fight for our Wotan and the New European Order.'

'And die for it.'

'And die for it,' von Dodenburg echoed. He slumped down on his stiff-backed chair and stared numbly at the draft's papers on the table in front of him. 'Now, perhaps you can guess Schulze why the Butcher Boy wanted that Ami tank stolen?' He looked up suddenly. 'What does it all add up to? I'll tell you. It means it won't be long before the Führer's Fire Brigade is back in action once again.'

Schulze stared down at his CO, aghast. 'Shit,' he breathed, 'shit, shit, shit.'

3

'*Shit!*' Major Harsch, the new commander of Wotan's panzer grenadiers, bellowed the word from a rat trap of a mouth that seemed to be worked by steel springs. 'If I tell you to shovel shit with your bare hands, you will do it!' His cold, unblinking eyes swept the stiff lines of volunteers drawn up in the snowy field behind the dirty white farmhouse. '*Do you understand?*'

'*We understand, Major!*' two hundred voices yelled back in unison, their breath fogging the icy morning air.

The tall major grunted in apparent satisfaction. 'German soldiers, folk comrades, you now have the honour of belonging to the SS's premier formation. The Wotan has fought on every battle front in Europe – the Low Countries, Russia, Italy, France – and has never yet been defeated. And why has the Wotan never been defeated? I shall tell you. Because its men know that their officers demand one hundred per cent blind unquestioning obedience from them.' The young Major suddenly screamed, '*Down!*'

The two hundred volunteers flopped on to the freezing snow as one and lay there rigidly like dead men, their arms pressed down their sides, still in the position of attention. Major Harsch let them lie there, his cold eyes searching the bare snowy horizon.

'*Up!*' he bellowed. In the stark black trees the crows rose, squawking their hoarse protests once again.

The panzer grenadiers, the fronts of their uniforms black with moisture, sprang to their feet, bodies freezing in the icy November wind.

Major Harsch slapped his riding crop against the side of his black-gleaming jackboot. 'That is what I want from you – unquestioning obedience – in the days to come. For comrades, there is no doubt that once our new secret weapons are put into operation, the Führer Adolf Hitler' – he said the name as if it were in italics – 'will grant the Wotan the great honour of going into action once more. When that day comes, I expect you to win me a regiment of my own and help me to cure my throat-ache.' He touched his throat to show that he meant the Knight's Cross, the high decoration he coveted. 'Even if you have to die in the attempt.'

'We understand, Major!'

Colonel von Dodenburg, shivering on the edge of the field in his black leather jacket, watched the New Major thoughtfully. Harsch had not yet been in combat. Throughout the war he had been a lieutenant in the Berlin Guard Battalion, concerned solely with ceremonial duties and parades. In the confusion of Generals' putsch the previous July,[1] however, Lieutenant Harsch had shown he was not lacking in initiative. He had taken it upon himself to surround the War Ministry in the *Bendlerstrasse* and had personally shot four generals and a field marshal implicated in the plot against Hitler's life. In return the Führer had awarded him the German Cross in Gold and transferred him to the Armed SS with the rank of major. Now, snatched from the obscurity of the Guards Battalion, it was obvious that Harsch, apparently unaware that the war was already lost, believed he could carve a glorious career for himself in Battle Group Wotan.

Colonel von Dodenburg sighed. Once he had been like the Major, keen, eager, ambitious, always ready to grab some desperate glory, prepared to die 'the hero's death' (as the press had it) for 'Führer, Folk and Fatherland'. But those days were long past; now he felt a hundred years old. He thrust his hands deep into his pockets and turning, crunched back across the white glare of the snowy field towards the warmth of his HQ.

Behind him the ambitious Major was bellowing: 'You think you are trained soldiers. But you're wrong. You're shitty greenbeaks, who don't know their arse from their elbow. Now you're really going to learn how to be a soldier. From now onwards it's going to be either march or croak. *What's it going to be, soldiers?*'

As a bowed-shouldered Colonel von Dodenburg opened the

[1] The July 1944 Army plot to assassinate Hitler. (*Transl.*)

door of his farmhouse HQ and felt the comforting warmth of the green-tiled stove in the corner strike his chilled peaked face, the volunteers' eager cracked voices floated across to him; '*March or croak!*'

* * *

Major Harsch set a tremendous pace. Every morning he would awake his command with a practice grenade through an open window and send the surprised youths fleeing through the deep snow in their bare feet, their nightshirts flapping around their knees. An hour later at the first parade he would announce, invariably: 'First exercise-up the hill. Live ammo! If I don't get at least one broken arm or a flesh wound, there'll be two hours' extra drill this afternoon. All right, snap to it!' And he would hasten the young giants, weighed down with thirty kilos of equipment, up the hill with a burst of fire from his machine-pistol, stitching the snow at their heels with red and white tracer.

Thereafter he would jeer and spit at the gasping, broken-lunged young soldiers, harrying and forcing them to greater efforts as they slogged through the waist-deep snow. He made them goose-step through an icy, squelching bog to the music of the First SS Corps' band. He forced them to crawl through a live minefield, with the unfortunate or unwary lying screaming in the snow behind the rest, clutching their ruined legs or blood-filled crotches. He ordered them to dig foxholes in the iron-hard earth and when they had done so, ran a 60-ton Tiger tank across their positions, churning up a great hail of earth and snow and leaving the young soldiers sobbing hysterically behind it in their holes, their grey trousers black where they had evacuated their bowels in fear. Within a week Major Josef Harsch had become the most hated man in SS Battle Group Wotan.

Sergeant Schulze, the Battle Group's most senior NCO, fell foul of him on the day after his arrival. He was having his morning break, sitting comfortably in the officers' latrine, jacket undone, a cup of red-hot nigger sweat in one hand, a tattered French pornographic magazine in the other, when the new Major strode in imperiously, already fumbling with his flies.

Starving Sepp, sitting in the next cubicle, bolted the rest of his sausage sandwich and sprang to attention, his ragged civilian pants falling around his skinny shanks. 'Attention, officer present!' he yelled in his strange Belgian accent.

The big Hamburger looked slowly up from a picture of two eton-cropped French ladies in their middle-forties doing something unpleasant to each other. Casually he raised his work-hardened fist to his brow.

Major Harsh choked. Stretching his neck out of his tight collar like a strangulated ostrich, he cried: 'How dare you? ... Salute me while you're sitting there ... *shitting*, with a dirty magazine in your big paw!' His voice rose hysterically and Starving Sepp, grinning wickedly behind his back, thought he might have a stroke at any moment. 'And in the officers' latrine, at that!'

Schulze was unmoved. He was an expert at officer-baiting; he had had five years' experience of it. 'I didn't know it was the officers' latrine, sir,' he said apologetically. 'It's my eyes, sir. The result of an old wound, you know. These days I've got to find my way around with the help of the old conk.' He touched his red drinker's nose by way of explanation. 'Blind as a bat. Now I can only tell where I am by the smell. Officer's shit seems to pong the same as that of the men—'

'Will you shut your filthy insubordinate mouth!' Harsch exploded. 'Now get to your feet, button up that jacket and salute correctly!'

Schulze didn't move.

'What's the matter with you, man?'

'Can't move, sir,' Schulze said easily.

'*Can't move!* Why in three devils' name, can't you move?' Harsch bellowed, while behind him Starving Sepp thrust his skinny fist into his mouth to prevent himself from laughing out loud.

It was just then that Colonel von Dodenburg appeared at the entrance to the latrine. He summed up the situation at once. Biting back his first impulse to laugh out loud, he snapped severely: 'Schulze, get yourself dressed and stand to attention when you speak to the Major.'

Dressing hurriedly and giving the crimson-faced young Major a good look at his broad chest covered in decorations, Schulze presented him with an immaculate salute. Von Dodenburg nodded approvingly. 'All right, you can go – and take that human scarecrow,' he indicated the Belgian, 'with you before he makes my bowels seize up.'

Von Dodenburg waited until the pair had vanished; then he turned to Harsch. 'One word of advice, Major,' he said. 'this is not the Berlin Guards' Battalion. This is the Wotan and we are at the front. Here experienced old NCOs like Schulze are worth a dozen majors – or colonels too, for that matter.' He smiled, but Harsch's hard face did not relax.

Von Dodenburg shrugged impatiently. 'See then, please, that you treat the NCOs accordingly.'

* * *

As November gave way to a hellishly cold December, a worried von Dodenburg noted the signs of a major build-up on all sides of the quiet Eifel front. Movable ramps were brought up during the cover of darkness, obviously for big tanks to cross the dragon's teeth of the West Wall, which ran the length of the Wotan's front. Behind their positions the pioneers laboured every night to build wooden roads through the thick Eifel forests, covering them with heavy beds of straw when they were finished, to deaden the metallic clank of tanks and infantry half-tracks.

A massive security clamp descended upon the SS Army, now assembling in the snow-bound forests. Radio silence was one hundred per cent. All messages of any importance were carried by taciturn officer couriers. Civilian phone traffic in the villages was monitored by the SD.[1] Each tiny tumbledown Eifel village was assigned a camouflage officer, who conscripted the old men and boys into work commandos for that purpose. The chain-dogs of the Field Gendarmerie were everywhere. Roll calls were made five or six times a day to prevent desertion.

[1] The SS's secret police. (*Transl.*)

And whenever the hard-faced chain-dogs did capture some unfortunate wretch of a deserter, he was strung up without trial on the nearest tree, and left there to swing back and forth in the December wind as a warning to the others.

Sergeant Schulze, his big bottom pressed against the comforting warmth of the HQ's green-tiled oven and a cup of nigger sweat in his fist, observed to Colonel von Dodenburg more than once: 'Sir, it won't be long now – and then the shit will hit the fan!'

It was a pessimistic forecast, with which the Wotan's CO could only agree.

On the 10th December 1944, the order came from the Sixth SS Panzer Army HQ at Bad Muenstereifel that all SS men in hospital who were not seriously incapacitated, would be returned to their units at once to fill the gaps in the panzer grenadier battalions. Regardless of their former speciality – tank driver, radioman, mechanic, gunner – they would all go to the infantry.

It happened that Schulze himself intercepted the message before it reached Major Harsch and as he read it, it dawned on him that one of the men who would be affected would be his side-kick Sergeant Matz, the one-legged monkey-faced tank driver, who had gone on leave to visit one of the various mistresses he had spread all over the Reich, and had not returned to Wotan. Instead he had been placed in the Military Hospital in nearby Dueren.

'By the great whore of Buxtehude,' exclaimed Schuze, startling Starving Sepp who was playing dice with Hairless Harry for his weekly ration of Old man, 'that bastard Harsch will get the fornicating little ape into his stubble-hoppers, if I don't warn him! Hey you,' he roared at Hairless Harry, 'get your lazy Belgie arse off'n that chair before I kick it off and start up the Volkswagen. We're off on a mission of mercy.'

* * *

Sergeant Matz was smoking a looted Ami cigar and drinking beer out of a big litre bottle when Schulze flung open the door with a loud, 'Hello, you old fart, strap on yer pegleg! I've got some good news for you, you cripple. You're discharged.' He stopped as he caught sight of the only other member of the little ward.

It was a man encased from head to toe in white plaster, all four limbs raised into the air by an intricate combination of weights and strings, with a jar on either side of him attached to the plaster by slim red rubber hoses. All that Schulze could see of the white figure was a dark frayed hole where the mouth might have been.

'What's that?' Schulze asked curiously. 'One of ours?'

Matz shook his head. 'Ner, that cow of a head nurse says he's from the *Wehrmacht*. Some stupid bastard of a stubble-hopper who got his eggs toasted by an Ami flame-thrower. That's what she says.' Matz blew out a contemptuous stream of blue smoke and Schulze noted for the first time that his gums were painted purple with gentian-violet solution. 'Me, I don't think there's anybody inside of it.' He flicked his ash off on the still white figure. 'Or if there is, he's been dead ever since I've been in here.'

'Oh,' Schulze lost interest and plumped himself down heavily on Matz's rumpled bed. 'And what you got, you rotten little cripple?'

'Pox,' Matz answered, 'a nice case of clap. A burst of it caught me while I was flying a low level attack over a blonde with big tits in *Planten un Bloomen*[1].' He smiled happily and took a slug of his beer. 'Keep me in here for another couple of shitting weeks at least. Might even spin it out till Christmas, if I'm lucky. The bone-patchers say they've never seen anybody like me who can piss five ways at once.'

Schulze grinned. 'No Christmas for you, mate. You've got to get that shitty leg of yours on and come with me. The Colonel needs you. Otherwise it's the stubble-hoppers for you, pegleg and all.'

A few minutes later the two SS NCOs were staggering into the grey December morning towards the waiting Volkswagen, where Starving Sepp was wolfing down a piece of white hospital bread, gunning the engine wildly. Matz flung his artificial

[1] A large park in the centre of Hamburg. (*Transl.*)

leg at Hairless Harry. 'Take care of that, will yer! And don't you dare lose it, or I'll have the eggs off you, if it's the last thing I do!'

Hairless Harry ducked as Schulze hurled Matz's boots into the back, diving after them at the same time as Starving Sepp let out the clutch. The Volkswagen shot forward, careened wildly to avoid the guard at the gate, waving his arms angrily for them to stop. A moment later they were on the main road heading out of Dueren back to the Eifel hills.

Colonel von Dodenburg himself was waiting for them as they drove across the urine-stained snow into the courtyard of his HQ. He was dressed in his best uniform, complete with all his decorations.

Schulze dropped out of the Volkswagen before it had stopped completely and swung him up an immaculate salute. 'I've brought Sergeant Matz back with me, sir. I gave him the instant cure for his complaint – a swift kick up the arse. But what's all the tin for, sir?' He indicated von Dodenburg's decorations.

'My dear Sergeant Schulze, you and I are going to pay a special visit. So get those rogues out of *my* Volkswagen. We have been summoned to pay a visit to the greatest captain of all times.'

'Oh my holy strawsack,' Schulze moaned. 'Not the Führer?'

'The very same – now will you get behind that wheel!'

4

'Gentlemen, the Führer Adolf Hitler!'

The divisional commanders of the Sixth SS Panzer Army and their staffs stiffened to attention. The great medieval hall of Ziegenberg Castle echoed and re-echoed to the harsh crunch of their polished high boots. They fixed their eyes expectantly on the high arched Gothic door, flanked by the tall black-clad SS officer adjutants, machine-pistols slung around their necks.

Slowly and shakily Adolf Hitler turned the corner, supported by Field Marshal Keitel and Colonel-General Jodl, his two chief military advisers.

'Heil Hitler!' bellowed Sepp Dietrich, Commander of the Sixth Army, at the top of his schnapps-thickened voice.

'Heil Hitler!' they roared back so that the black rafters in the grey Gothic gloom above them trembled with the sound.

The head of the Thousand Year Empire flipped his right arm up in acknowledgement and said softly. 'Thank you, gentlemen. But please be seated. I have something of great importance to say to you all.'

The brass settled themselves with a shuffle of feet in the high wooden chairs, while the giant adjutants crooked their fingers over the triggers of their mps, alert for any attempt on the Führer's life.

Adolf Hitler's left arm trembled uncontrollably as he stared at these men who commanded and would lose a million of his elite troops. To von Dodenburg he looked burned out, an old, crippled man who would not live much longer. Was this the man to whom Germany's fate should be entrusted at this moment of ultimate crisis?

But as soon as the German Leader spoke his opening words, von Dodenburg knew that he had not lost his old power to shock and dramatize. 'Gentlemen,' he announced, his voice low and hoarse, 'On December 16th 1944, the German armies in the West will once again go over to the offensive!'

There was a sudden excited buzz of chatter among the generals.

Hitler held up his hand for silence. 'At five thirty precisely on that morning, gentlemen, the Seventh Infantry, the Fifth Panzer and your own Sixth SS Panzer Armies will attack the Western Allies on the Ardennes front between Monschau and Echternach, seventy kilometres of front held by four weak American divisions. General von Manteuffel's Fifth on your left flank will have the objective of capturing St Vith and pushing on into Luxembourg. To his left General Brandeberger's Seventh will seize the Vianden-Echternach area and guard Manteuffel's flank. Hitler paused and licked the spittle from his lips. 'You, my dear SS generals of the Sixth will have the most important task, however. With four panzer divisions and five infantry, you will attack from Moschau to the Losheim Gap, smash through the enemy line, head for the Meuse and once across the river,' his voice rose excitedly, 'you will drive for Antwerp and capture it!'

Von Dodenburg felt his heart sink as he watched the colour flush the Führer's sallow face. Antwerp! It was an impossible objective.

'Once we have captured the enemy's major supply port,' Hitler continued 'and divided the English and American armies, the Anglo-Americans will be forced to sue for a separate peace. Our Intelligence tells us that the British are already scraping the manpower barrel and as you all know the Amis have no heart for fighting. Then, gentlemen,' he concluded grimly, 'we shall deal with the Russians once and for all, that I can promise you on my holy oath!'

In the stunned silence that had suddenly descended upon the conference, Hitler slumped down into the chair that two of the gigantic adjutants pushed beneath his frail body. For a long moment, nobody moved, nobody spoke. In the flickering light of the candles they seemed frozen there eternally, their wavering shadows thrown grotesquely on the bare cold walls.

Jodl broke the spell. He cleared his throat and said drily,

'Gentlemen, I wonder if I could have your attention for a few facts and figures? 77,000 replacements fed into the three armies . . . 3.17 million litres of fuel . . . each tank with fuel for one hundred and twenty kilometres . . . eight days' supply of ammunition on hand . . . three hundred fifty fighters in support, including eighty of the new jets . . . a quarter of a million German soldiers in the line, facing an estimated 80,000 Americans . . .'

Figure after figure, in that dry precise cynical voice of his, while von Dodenburg's brain reeled. Where had Germany obtained so many men and so much material at this desperate stage of the war he asked himself time and time again.

Adolf Hitler himself answered that question when Jodl was finally finished his exposé. Helped to his feet by two of the black-clad adjutants, he took off the nickel-framed spectacles with which he had been following the figures on the paper in front of him and said, 'Gentlemen, this great new offensive has only been made possible by the last, superhuman effort of our folk comrades in the factories and workshops of the Reich. They will never be able to make the same effort again. Before you go your separate ways for your briefings, I would like you all to bear this in mind. This battle is to decide whether we shall live or die. I want all my soldiers to fight hard and without pity. The battle must be fought with brutality and all resistance must be broken in a wave of terror. In this most grave hour of the Fatherland, I expect every one of my soldiers to be courageous and courageous once again.' His voice rose to an hysterical scream as it had done in the tremendous days of the pre-war Party Rallies, '*The enemy must be beaten – now or never! Otherwise our Germany dies!*'

* * *

'Well,' asked General Kraemer, Dietrich's cynical sophisticated Chief-of-Staff of a still shaken von Dodenburg, 'what did you think of the Old Man's performance?'

Behind them in the echoing ante-room which had been laid out with maps for the briefing, the 'Butcher Boy' was drinking looted American Army scotch, his favourite, with the commanders of the 'Bodyguard' and the 'Hitler Youth' Divisions.

'Tremendous,' von Dodenburg stuttered. 'But are those figures Jodl quoted true?'

Kraemer placed a perfumed Turkish cigarette in his ivory cigarette holder with carefully manicured and polished fingers, 'Of course. Jodl is a cunning fox, I'll give you that, but he's honest – or as honest as we all are these days.' Kraemer blew a careful smoke ring and leaned over the big map of the Ardennes spread out in front of him on the great oaken table. 'You, my dear von Dodenburg, have been accorded a great honour by the Führer.' Kraemer poked a finger at the map. 'The Losheim Gap – the classic invasion route west, as I am sure you will recollect from your military history classes – will be forced, on the morning of the sixteenth, by two infantry divisions, the Third Para and the Twelfth People's Grenadier. Once the Ami crust is broken by them, your Battle Group will move through. At first the going will be tough – the roads are very tight for your Royal Tigers. But once you're over the River Salm, you'll have put those damned awkward Ardennes valleys behind you. At Werbomont, you'll join the motor road – that should be on the evening of the second day.' He straightened up and smoothed his elegant jacket. 'By the afternoon of the third, my dear von Dodenburg, the greatest captain of all time expects you to be in position to capture the bridge at Huy. From thence the infantry will head northeast for Antwerp and the war will be won!' He blew another careful smoke ring.

Von Dodenburg took his gaze from the big map. 'But General,' he protested, 'that route is not big enough for a bicyle, never mind a tank – and my Royal Tigers are seventy-two tonners!'

'I know, my dear boy,' Kraemer answered easily. 'As our noble army commander has put it in his own inimitable way. "That route is not big enough to fart on properly." But the Führer picked it for you personally. You must stick to Route B or you will snarl up the whole advance – and remember we have nine divisions – some 120,000 men – involved.'

Von Dodenburg bit his bottom lip and stared down at the

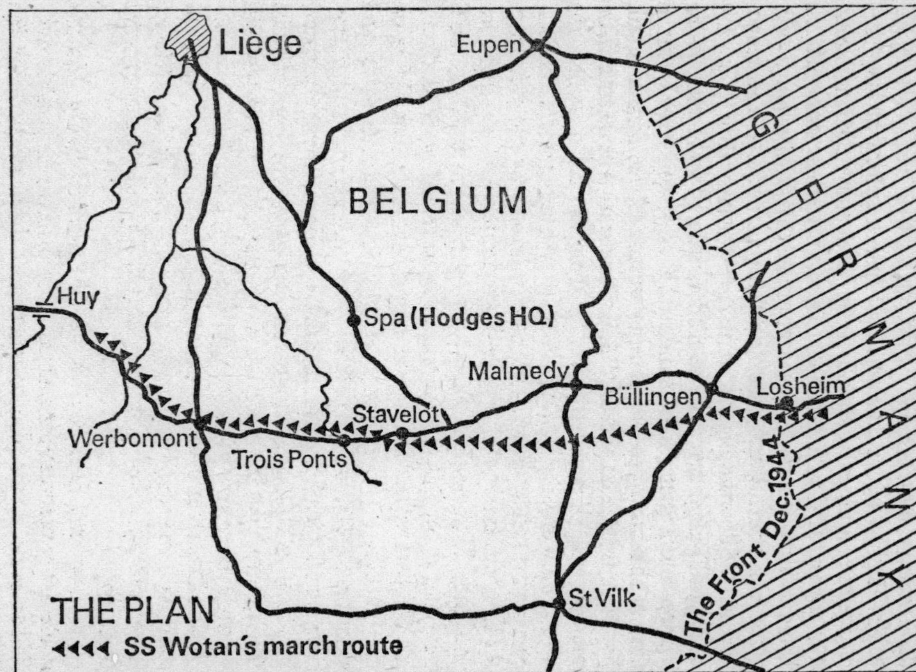
Liège
Eupen
GERMANY
BELGIUM
Huy
Spa (Hodges HQ)
Malmedy
Büllingen
Losheim
Stavelot
Werbomont
Trois Ponts
The Front Dec. 1944
St Vilk
THE PLAN
SS Wotan's march route

mass of blue marks indicating the American front line positions, the yellow flickering light hollowing out his handsome young face, making it appear almost wolfish. With only 5,000 men, admittedly Germany's best in this fifth year of war, he would have to break through them to a depth of at least ten kilometres. And even then, in the Ardennes' tight winding mountain roads, a handful of determined men armed with machine-guns, a few mines, and an anti-tank gun could still effectively hold his advance. Suddenly he recalled the stolen Ami tank. Subterfuge would have to be the answer.

General Kraemer seemed to read his mind. 'Von Dodenburg, I don't care a damn how you do it. Even if you've only got a platoon of panzer grenadiers and one tank left when you get to that Huy Bridge on the third day. But do it! The Meuse with one tank, von Dodenburg – that's all I ask of you!'

5

But von Dodenburg's hesitancy about the Führer's great new offensive was transformed into burning hatred of the Americans by what happened two days before the attack was destined to start.

At four on the morning of the 14th December, he was awakened roughly by a shaken, half-dressed Schulze pulling urgently at his naked arm. 'Colonel . . . Colonel, wake up for Christ's sake! *Wake up!*'

Colonel von Dodenburg fought his way out of the great two-metre high steel mousetrap, which in his nightmare had him pinned down on a narrow winding Ardennes valley-road, littered with the bloody bodies of young men in the field-grey of the SS. 'What is it?' he called in alarm through scummed lips, sweeping the sweat-matted blond hair from his damp brow. He stared up at Schulze's broad face, illuminated in the hissing white light of a captured Ami Coleman lamp.

Schulze gasped. 'It's HQ, sir. We've got to report to Dueren at once. A thousand bomber attack by the Amis. They've knocked the shit out of the place! Dueren doesn't exist any more!'

* * *

The Flying Fortresses had gone. But the centre of Dueren, the Sixth Army's vital railhead, was still a sea of searing red flame, as the long Wotan convoy started to nose its way cautiously through the smouldering suburbs, stopping continually to avoid the bodies which lay sprawled carelessly everywhere.

A roof collapsed and a shower of angry sparks smothered the men in the open Volkswagen jeep leading the convoy. Its occupants ducked instinctively and, in his fright, Starving Sepp, sitting next to Matz, the driver, let go of the carrot he had been gnawing.

'Sweet shit!' cursed Schulze, beating out the sparks on his jacket, 'that was fucking close.'

A line of civilians, naked and barefoot, bodies smeared with blood and soot, the newly blind and the lame supporting each other the best they could, clawed at the sides of the Volkswagen as it crawled past. To a shocked von Dodenburg they looked like figures from some medieval portrait of the victims of the Black Death.

'Jesus, Mary, Joseph,' Starving Sepp crossed himself.

'Oh, my aching arse,' groaned Schulze, 'this is worse than Hamburg in July 1943.'[1]

The road narrowed, hemmed in on both sides by piles of brick rubble and grotesquely twisted iron girders. Matz changed down and prepared to drive over the body of a young woman in a flowered cotton dress who barred the centre of the street.

Von Dodenburg grabbed his shoulder. 'No, not over her,' he cried, his face twisted in horror.

'I'll fix it,' Schulze yelled above the roar, glancing away from his CO's tortured face.

As he dropped over the side, a stream of rats streamed out of some cellar or other in front of his feet. He aimed an angry kick at them, and bent down over the young housewife's body. Her eyes were wildly staring; her face like a soft shelled egg. He had seen the like in Hamburg the year before. Beneath the skin every bone would be crushed. Fighting back his desire to vomit, Schulze bent down to pick her up and deposited her at the side of the road.

And there was worse to come. Human trunks without arms or legs. Men, women and children shrunk by the searing flame to the size of pygmies. Dead civilians piled metre deep. Children, sobbing with terror, hopping along on their mangled limbs like wounded rabbits. Women, eyes bulging out of their sockets, newly white hair standing on end as they screamed. Old men cowering in terror, coughing with the stench as if their lungs would burst.

[1] Reference to the week-long air raid on Hamburg of that month. (*Transl.*)

Von Dodenburg was filled with hatred. Wildly he stared at the burning fiery sky and shook his fist at it, as if the young Ami pilots were up there, listening to him. 'In three devils' names,' he swore violently, his handsome young face etched into a death's head by the flames of dying Dueren, 'I'll castrate you Ami bastards before I'm finished – *every single one of you . . .*'

6

The officers, non-commissioned officers and men of Wotan – old sweats and fresh young greenbeaks alike – celebrated their last night before the great new offensive in the West in the elite unit's traditional fashion: by getting blind, roaring paralytically drunk.

In the sergeant's wet canteen, Schulze, red-faced, and happy at the prospect of the evening's fun, began the proceedings with one of his celebrated farts, which drew immediate laughter and applause from his comrades crowding the long, white scrubbed tables laden with bottles of cheap black market *Korn.*

'Silence in the whore-house!' Schulze roared. With lightning speed he downed the glass of *Korn* he held in each hamlike fist and bellowed the traditional command of that year of defeat, 1944: 'Lads, you better buy combs – lousy times are ahead!'

The NCOs sprang to their feet as one – the one-legged Sergeant Matz, the villainous-looking Sergeant Ochmann, an eye-patch covering his empty right socket, Sergeant Gross who made a habit of chewing razor-blades when he was drunk, which was most of the time, Sergeant Gierig whose face looked like a wrinkled pink prune thanks to an Ivan flamethrower, and a dozen other veterans of every battle front in Europe – and raised their schnapps glasses.

'*Buy combs – lousy times are ahead!*' they bellowed with hoarse enthusiasm and sank the fiery *Korn* in one quick gulp.

Schulze clapped the tight, black-silk-clad buttocks of the wet canteen manager's wife who was passing with her tray of glasses held high above her ample bosom. 'Come on, mother, let's get that beer flowing! We ain't got much time left. And remember the pea soup at midnight! We need plenty of ammo for our fart cannons! If we can't shoot the Amis, then at least we'll gas them to death with our green smoke. *Prost!*'

'*Prost!*' his comrades yelled back and raised their big one-litre beer bottles in toast. The big booze-up started.

* * *

But Colonel von Dodenburg was in no mood for celebrating. He wandered dutifully into the soldiers' mess, had a beer with them and laughed at the old soldiers' jokes about 'the second thing a soldier does when he comes home on leave to his missus is to take off his pack'. For a couple of minutes he watched Schulze's disgraceful drunken antics in the NCOs' wet canteen, which showed little respect for either Folk, Führer or Fatherland. With a forced smile on his tired face, he sipped a cognac with Major Harsch. Finally he excused himself with the traditional, 'Gentlemen, I should like to recommend myself. It's going to be a long day tomorrow and when you're as old as I am, you need your sleep!'

The drunken young men clicked their highly polished jack-boots together, discipline reasserting itself immediately. Almost casually he touched his hand to the peak of his elegant black cap with its shining death's head. 'Please stand at ease. And remember – up the cups, the night's going to be cold!'

Laughing uproariously, they raised their glasses to the level of their third tunic button, elbow held rigidly at right angle to the body, as they had been taught to do at their cadet schools in Bad Toelz and Brunswick.

Von Dodenburg standing at the door, ready to push aside the black-out curtain nodded. They raised the glasses as one to their lips. '*Up the cups, the night's going to be cold!*' they shouted with youthful enthusiasm. Then they had drained the glasses and threw them from all sides into the great empty marble fireplace. With the faint forced smile set on his lips, Colonel von Dodenburg passed out into the brilliant silver winter night to leave his command to celebrate without him.

But the young CO could not sleep. Tossing and turning miserably in his narrow cot, trying to force himself not to listen to the drunken bass singing coming from the sergeants' wet canteen, he simply could not stop his mind racing with the details of the new offensive: POL, 88 mm shell supplies, food, routes, running times – the hundred and one technical details upon which the success of his drive for the bridge at Huy depended.

Again he ran his mind over the tortuous mountainous route he would have to take through the Ardennes before he reached his objective. Could the Tigers do it? What if they burnt up more fuel than Jodl anticipated? At four litres to a kilometre, that could easily be possible. Where would he find fuel then – with his administrative tail way back somewhere in rear-stallion land? What, too, if Jodl had misjudged the strength of the Amis' reaction to the surprise attack? He had done it before – at Kursk, Cassino, Aachen[1] – and Wotan had paid for it with their blood. If the Amis had their infantry in the Ardennes in any strength, his sixty-ton Tigers, protected only by a handful of inexperienced panzer grenadiers, would be at the mercy of their anti-tank guns in the tight little Belgian valleys with no room to manoeuvre.

Thus the questions raced back and forth through his mind – questions that could only be answered on the morrow in blood – until finally the Colonel drifted off into an uneasy sleep.

* * *

Senior Sergeant Schulze and his running-mate Sergeant Matz were too drunk and too randy to be plagued by doubts at that particular moment. Forage caps on the backs of their tousled heads, tunics ripped open at the neck, reeking of *Korn*, and holding bottles of beer in both hands, they staggered into the little town's one and only whorehouse, shoving aside the young soldiers who milled everywhere.

'Make way for a senior naval officer with a list to port!' yelled Matz, pushing past a burly People's Grenadier with the silver wound medal and the bronze badge of the combat infantryman. 'Where's the tail in this Holy Catholic whorehouse?' He laughed until the People's Grenadier hit him in the face with a dirty fist and sent him hurtling through the crowd.

[1] See *Claws of Steel*, *Guns at Casino*, *The Devil's Shield* for further details. (*Transl.*)

'Crappy SS,' the big stubble-hopper growled. 'Think they own the shitting show!'

'Yeah, yeah,' agreed a bunch of his comrades from the People's Grenadier Division. 'The likes of us does the shitting fighting and those asparagus Tarzans get all the credit.'

Schulze feigned drunken humility. 'But you see,' he said softly, keeping his gaze fixed on the dirty cigarette-littered floor of the brothel so that the Grenadiers could not see the look in his blood-shot eyes. 'That poor little feller is a cripple. Lost his leg fighting for your Folk Comrades against the nasty Ivans.'

The big Grenadier sneered and put his hand round a fat whore in red panties. 'Tough tittie,' he said. 'I'll start crying soon.'

'Tut-tut,' Schulze said, shaking his head. 'How cruel you chaps in the infantry are . . . Come on, Matz, let me help you to your feet.'

As he extended a hand to the little one-legged NCO sprawled in the corner, he winked.

Matz's face was shielded by Schulze's massive shape as his mouth framed the word 'NOW'. Schulze nodded and heaved. An instant later, a beer bottle flew through the air and shattered just above the Grenadier's head, splattering him with beer and glass.

The whores screamed. A fat, blonde madam yelled something about the 'chain-dogs' until one of the Grenadiers jabbed his elbow into her belly and she doubled up like a deflated barrage balloon.

'So, that's the way it's going to be,' the big Grenadier said, slowly wiping the beer off his scarred face. 'You saw that lads, didn't you? A completely unprovoked act of violence at a time when any decent chap is thinking of higher things only.' He gestured up above, whence tiny drops of plaster were falling like snow while in one of the upstairs rooms, a sex-starved young soldier was making the bed springs sing squeakily.

'Yeah,' agreed one of his comrades from the People's Grenadier Division, slowly winding his leather belt round his fist, so that the silver buckle and its '*God with Us*' motto was on top, 'some people would fart in a house of God. Let's get the SS bastards!'

In that instant, Schulze heaved and picked up the whore in the red pants. She screamed as she flew through the air and landed, bottom first, right in the Grenadier's face. He went down as if he had been pole-axed.

'That'll learn yer not to take the holy name of Wotan in vain!' yelled Schulze exultantly as the mass of cursing, punching red-faced People's Grenadiers descended upon them and the battle began. Thus those men of the Wotan who were still on their feet celebrated in 'traditional fashion' their last night of 'peace' before the great offensive.

* * *

Colonel von Dodenburg woke to a grey, harsh December dawn, with the fog curling around their hutted camp like a soft-furred cat. Hollow-eyed and heavy-headed, he lay there in his narrow cot, listening to the sounds of a barracks coming to life: the hoarse caw-caw of the crows in the stark trees; the clatter of the kitchen-bulls at their goulash cannon in the kitchen; the warm hiss of some sentry or other relieving himself against a wall as he paused in his round; the harsh stamp of the duty NCO's winter-hard boots as he marched from hut to hut to waken the still drunk soldiers; their cries of protest and catcalls as he bellowed the traditional formula: 'all right, there, you bunch of asparagus Tarzans, hands off yer cocks and on with yer socks! Let's be having yer now'; the thick asthmatic sound of a truck being started in the chill dawn air—

Suddenly his train of thought was rudely disturbed by a drunken howling coming from the direction of the main gate, followed a moment later by a gruff command to be quiet. Curious, Colonel von Dodenburg sprang out of bed and rubbing a hole free in the frost-glazed window, gazed out at the scene at the gate.

Sergeants Schulze and Matz were swaying back and forth drunkenly at the red and white pole surrounded by half a dozen suspicious chain-dogs, hands clenched on their pistol holsters, while the young duty officer signed for them.

Von Dodenburg shook his head in dismay. 'No,' he groaned to himself, 'not that!'

Despite the freezing cold, Schulze was naked save for his boots, belt and what appeared to be a pair of frilly red lace panties which he wore jauntily on his head in lieu of the official off-duty forage cap. Matz, for his part, was carrying his artificial leg over his shoulder like a rifle and attempting to drink what his CO hoped was beer from a large ornate chamber-pot.

The chain-dogs were satisfied at last and, snapping to attention, they swung round and marched back to the truck in which they had brought their prisoners from Madam Sissy's brothel '*The Crazy Blue Ox*', leaving the confused young duty officer to deal with the two drunken NCOs. But Schulze solved his problem for him. He grabbed Matz and raising his hand to the flaming red panties in salute, he said thickly to the wide-eyed young officer, 'Better get him back to barracks.' He winked conspiratorially. 'The poor little crippled bastard is drunk you know sir.'

Before anyone could stop them, the two veterans started to stagger off to their own quarters and as they did so, Schulze caught sight of the CO peering out at him from the frost-bound window. He flung him a tremendous salute, almost falling over in the attempt, a beatific grin on his drunken Hamburg face.

'Morning, sir,' he yelled at the top of his voice, sending the crows rising in hoarse protest from their perches, 'better buy combs – lousy times are ahead!'

Laughing uproariously, with Matz hopping beside him like a sparrow and still attempting to drink from the ornate chamber pot, the two of them disappeared towards their barracks . . .

7

It was zero five hours on the morning of December 16th 1944, and the Ardennes front was silent. Above the fir-spiked hill range, which marked the old frontier between Belgium and National Socialist Germany, the stars were cruel in the sparkling silver sky. But down below in the still sleeping Belgian valleys, the American positions were wreathed in a thick pre-dawn fog.

The fog was a stroke of good luck for the thousands of German soldiers waiting for the order to launch their last surprise attack of the war in the west. It deadened the hard metallic noise the tankers made, as they prepared for that moment when the engines of their Tigers must burst into noisy life. It muted the clank the gunners made as they unloaded and reloaded their cannon to check that the breeches had not frozen up; it muffled the soft persistent shuffle of the youthful white-clad assault infantry as they ploughed through the knee-deep snow in their jumping-off positions overlooking the valleys.

Shivering in the pre-dawn cold, the young panzer grenadiers crowded round Major Harsch and listened with growing excitement as he read them Field Marshal von Rundstedt's last message: 'Soldiers of the Western Front! Your great hour has come, great attack armies start against the Anglo-Americans. I do not have to tell you more than that. You feel it yourself. We gamble everything! You carry with you the holy obligation to give all to achieve superhuman objectives for our Fatherland and Führer!'

Schulze, standing on the turret of the captured Sherman which was manned by the two Belgian guides and driven by Matz, and which would lead Wotan's drive, stared down at von Dodenburg's thin pensive face. Somehow he sensed that the CO was sad as well as excited; sad at the thought of how many of the eager young panzer grenadiers would be dead before the coming battle was over.

As he kicked Matz's shoulder to indicate that he should start up, Schulze yelled across to von Dodenburg: 'Bye, Colonel, see you soon in America!'

Colonel von Dodenburg laughed and waved. The next instant the Sherman's 300 hp engine burst into violent life. Behind it the great 72-ton Royal Tigers did the same. The panzer grenadiers sprang into their half-tracks. To the left and right in the snowy, blue-lit fields, the gunnery officers raised their right arms, eyes fixed on the luminous dials of their watches. Silently their lips moving but emitting no sound, they began to count away the seconds. Ten . . . nine . . . eight . . . seven

It was five thirty. Their arms cracked down. 'FIRE!' they yelled.

All along the Sixth SS Panzer Army's front, hundreds of guns, mortars, rocket launchers crashed into action. With a hoarse scream, their shells sped towards the sleeping Americans' positions. The last offensive had begun.

TWO: A BRIDGE AT HUY

'When this battle is over, I want that guy Dodenburg's head brought to me on a goddam silver platter!'

General Dwight D. Eisenhower,
17th December, 1944.

I

Saturday, December 16th 1944.

In the valley the snow was coming down softly and sadly now, deadening a little the steady roar of the guns at the front. Here and there a GI crouched over a blue-smoking fire of wet twigs trying to dry his damp socks while the tears from the smoke stung his eyes. Others smoked apathetically, worn out by the long day's rumours and counter-rumours about the German breakthrough up the line. A few lined up in front of the kitchen trucks in the centre of the valley, mess tins in hand, staring dully at the blue gasoline lights underneath the ash barrels of boiling water, waiting for the usual luke-warm, wet hash and a canteen cup of coffee.

'You see guys,' explained the little first Lieutenant with the sinus trouble. 'We're here in Belgium.' He drew a line in the snow with an abandoned bayonet. 'And the Heinies are here. Now in this spot here – the Losheim gap, they call it.' He drew an arrow, 'the enemy's pouring through. But no sweat. Our guys are getting ready to really smack the Kraut where it hurts.'

'What guys, Lieutenant?' interrupted a GI with a khaki blanket wrapped around his helmeted head. 'We ain't seen nobody up there in them hills all day long.' He indicated the front with a nod of his blanketed head.

'Yeah, yeah, Short-Ass is right, Lieutenant!' a chorus of voices agreed.

'But you see . . .' the harassed company commander began. He never completed the sentence.

Next to the steaming boilers, a fat cook with a dirty stained towel wrapped round his belly started to strike the warning triangle, shouting in a tough Brooklyn accent, 'Okay, you chowhounds come and get it. Chow's up!'

'Chow's up!' the men echoed the call and began to push their

way down the snow trail, leaving the Lieutenant standing there without an audience.

The cooks were nervous – the infantrymen could see that. They hurried the hungry troops down the line, slapping the hash carelessly into their mess tins, slopping the coffee into their canteen cups with trembling hands.

'What's up with you hashslingers?' quipped a GI. 'You look as if yer gonna cream yer skivvies any minute. The lousy krauts ain't just over the other side of that hill, ya know.'

'That's what you think,' one of the cooks replied darkly. 'You ain't seen what's going on back of the line like we have. The whole goddam front's bugging out. There ain't enough room to fart on them roads back there. The whole of Eighth Corps is moving out – and we're stuck out here like a spare penis at a wedding. All the smart guys,' he added bitterly, 'have already bugged. We're the fall guys—we're for the chop—'

'All right, Smithers, knock it off, will ya!' cut in Sergeant Abe Rosenbloom, the heavy-shouldered, dark-jowled, fat head cook. 'What do you want these guys to do – cry into their hash? Now move it and get that Java served!'

The line started to move forward more swiftly, as the cooks redoubled their efforts to get rid of the food and be off. Already those of them who had finished cooking were dousing their fires and loading up the waiting jeeps, the drivers gunning their engines, clouding the icy air with dark blue smoke. Others were rolling up the cooking equipment as fast as they could. Their haste affected the infantrymen standing out in the snow, spooning down their food. They began to gulp it down swiftly and double over to the impatient line in front of boiling tubs of water, waiting to clean their mess tins.

To Sergeant Rosenbloom, the head cook, the rush and excitement seemed like a circus he had once seen as a kid, breaking up in a hurry to beat a bad storm. Rosenbloom, a peacetime short-order cook in a Brooklyn hamburger heaven, had an uneasy feeling that something unpleasant was going to happen soon and he wanted his men out and back on the road to St Vith and safety. 'Let's go,' he chivvied, 'Let's go, guys! We ain't got all goddam day.'

It was just then that the strange Sherman breasted the height above them. The snow had deadened the sound of its approach. Now, suddenly, it teetered there, while the GIs below, frozen into abrupt immobility, stared at it, open mouths full of hash. With a throaty roar of its 300 hp engine, it began to roll slowly downwards, straight towards them.

'It's one of ours, guys,' yelled the Lieutenant with the sinus trouble reassuringly. 'Relax it!'

'I can't see any unit insignia, Lieutenant,' a bearded sergeant answered uncertainly, reaching for his 45 with his free hand. 'Not hair nor hide of it!'

Standing next to the boilers, Sergeant Rosenbloom unconsciously began to grip the cook's ladle he was holding, like a weapon, as the sinister Sherman rumbled closer. Still no one moved. Behind him a freckled-faced teenage GI, eyes wide and staring, was whistling *'I'm Dreaming of a White Christmas'* monotonously through a gap in his front teeth.

When the Sherman was only a hundred yards away it braked to a stop in a flurry of soft snow. Slowly, with no sound save the soft hum of the electric turret motor, the long overhanging 75 mm gun began to swing round in their direction.

'What the hell's that guy up to?' cried the freckled-faced kid in alarm.

'Run for it,' yelled the Lieutenant with the sinus trouble. *'It's a Kraut!'*

CRRR-ACK. The 75 mm opened up. HE exploded in white fury among their massed ranks. Men fell everywhere. *'Medic ... medic, get me outa here!'* the wounded screamed hysterically on all sides in the scorched snow. The Sherman fired again. Behind it on the ridge, dark little figures in the camouflaged smocks of the SS were streaming out of the snow-heavy firs, firing from the hip with their automatics as they stumbled down the slope.

Sergeant Rosenbloom dropped his ladle. He spun round. The GIs had broken, throwing away their weapons, screaming at the tops of their voices, they were running for the cover of the wood behind them. For a moment he hesitated.

The 75 mm shell exploded only twenty yards away. Snow

plummeted upwards. Fist-sized, razor-edged shards of metal hissed through the air. Men screamed and dropped in their tracks, nursing wounded arms, staring numbly at severed legs, silent for good, sprawled out violently in the red snow.

The fat cook started to run awkwardly. Angry slugs stitched a pattern in the snow at his heels as he blundered blindly through the bushes. Next to him a thin pine snapped and crashed into the snow. He dodged it just in time. Ahead of him he could see a grove of tall pines, thickly grouped together. If he could make them, he would be safe. Summoning up the last of his strength, he vaulted over the body of a GI sprawling in the snow and pelted desperately towards the trees. Others had spotted the same cover. Thirty yards to go . . . twenty . . . they were nearly there now. A vicious burst of machine-gun fire caught the men at the rear of the fleeing group. Fifteen yards to go now!

Rosenbloom, his lungs wheezing, told himself they were going to make it. Ten yards and – With a crash, a great monster of a tank thrust its snout through the pines, sending them keeling over on all sides, showering it with wild flurries of snow. But despite the snow, Sergeant Abe Rosenbloom could not mistake the harsh black and white iron cross on its side. As the turret flapped open and the dark-uniformed figure holding a Schmeisser machine-pistol came into view, he started slowly to raise his hands. All around him the terrified survivors of what had once been an infantry company were doing the same, their wide eyes taking in the silver runic double 'S' on the man's collar and all it implied. The Jewish Sergeant-Cook was a prisoner of the SS.

* * *

'Will you just look at the skinny Belgie bastard,' Schulze chuckled at Matz and Colonel von Dodenburg as they stood on the turret of the Royal Tiger eating the captured U.S. hash from the cans, 'it's like giving a shitty elephant a strawberry! You just can't satisfy the greedy sod!' He indicated Starving Sepp with his hash-laden spoon.

Von Dodenburg laughed easily and tossed the rest of his can

over the side of the turret. 'Leave him in peace, Schulze,' he said. 'We're going to need our friend before this campaign is over. He knows these backroads like he does the inside of his own pocket. Let him stuff his guts if he wants to – there are going to be lean times ahead as it is.'

But despite this warning comment, Colonel von Dodenburg was satisfied with the progress of the first day of the new offensive so far. The Sixth SS Army's two lead infantry divisions had forced the Losheim Gap easily enough. The raw American troops guarding the classic route west had broken and run almost at once, streaming back from the front in their thousands. Wotan had followed into the gap, without firing a single shot. There was only one fly in the ointment. Wotan was running out of 'Otto'.

'Schulze,' snapped von Dodenburg as Harsch's panzer grenadiers started to herd what was left of the overrun American company into the centre of a square formed by their half tracks, 'what's the fuel situation?'

Schulze thrust his big thumb downwards. 'Not so rosy, sir. We've got plenty of gas for the Sherman. But we're down to about ten kilometres running-time for the Tigers. These shitty Belgie hills certainly hit fuel consumption.'

Von Dodenburg absorbed the disquieting information with a curt nod. It was what he expected. Otto was running out and they had hardly started on their mission. The planners at Ziegenberg had slipped up badly; they had not calculated how much the rugged snowy Ardennes terrain would eat up of the vital two days' supply of diesel and gasoline. But what was he to do? Could he afford to wait until the urgently needed supplies caught up with him? It took him only a moment's deliberation to realize that he couldn't. Every hour was vital if he were to seize the key bridge by the third day. He had to find fuel elsewhere.

For a moment he stared at the Ami POWs. With their khaki blankets drawn over their heads against the soft gentle snow, they looked like doomed men on their way to be executed. *Poor bastards,* he muttered softly to himself. He caught the eye of one of them – a fat man with sergeant's stripes on his arms.

The man, who looked like a *Stürmer*[1] caricature of a Jew, was staring at him fiercely, as if he could barely restrain himself from springing forward and wrapping his big greasy hands around the German officer's throat.

Von Dodenburg turned and called, 'Harsch – Major Harsch – could I speak to you?'

Abe Rosenbloom, now minus the silver watch he had received for his Bar Mizavah and the pen his mother had given him when he had been drafted, stared angrily at the handsome young SS Colonel towering above him. In the past his private code of conduct had always read – when the shit is about to hit the fan, the innocent should leave the room double-quick. But now, despite his fear of the SS men, he was consumed by a burning hatred of the apparently confident young Colonel. 'Just you wait, you German bastard, I'll fix your heels for you one of these days!' he hissed.

Colonel von Dodenburg, unaware of Rosenbloom, was conferring with the panzer grenadier CO, his head bent over the map. 'You see, Harsch, this is the Reich's line-of-march – Route A – running through Buellingen and the nearest Ami POL dump[2] – three kilometres from here, that's all.'

Harsch looked at him aghast. 'But, Colonel, General Dietrich gave a specific order that we must not use any other division's line of advance.'

Von Dodenburg grinned. 'My dear Major, I can see you have not been at the front long. Generals and all the rest of the base stallions give a lot of orders *behind* the line. What happens *up* in the line is something quite different. Besides,' the Colonel continued, 'those ruptured ducks of the Reich[3] are always behind schedule. We could be into that depot, grab what we want and be back on Route B before the Reich even knows we've been and gone.' He wiped the soft snow from his face. 'If we wait, the Amis could well blow the place up and then nobody gets the fuel. Now what I suggest is that I take a small party from the point, the Sherman, my jeep, a Tiger and a couple of half

[1] Anti-semitic Nazi paper. (*Transl.*)
[2] Fuel Dump. (*Transl.*)
[3] Reich Division, Wotan's SS panzer running-mate. (*Transl.*)

tracks with your grenadiers. The front runners can guide us through the forest trails to Buellingen. With a bit of luck, we'll be able to rush the place before the Ami knows what's hit him. I'll signal you – codeword 'Otto' – and you'll come up at the double with the rest of Wotan. If luck's on our side, we'll be cleared of the place before the Reich's point approaches it.' He grinned suddenly. 'I'd like to see their mugs when they find out we've beaten them to the loot.'

Harsch swung his head towards the shivering Ami prisoners-of-war. 'And that rabble of Jews, gangsters and cowboys?' he queried stiffly. 'What am I to do with them when we move off?'

Von Dodenburg shrugged easily. 'I can leave you with that problem, can't I Harsch?'

Harsch's cold eyes flickered momentarily; then his jaws snapped, 'Yes, I can take care of them, Colonel.'

'Good.'

As Colonel von Dodenburg set about organizing his raiding party, he little realized that the simple suggestion, uttered so casually, would haunt him for the rest of his life.

* * *

It was just after three now. The snow had stopped. But a grey, damp fog was beginning to swirl in from the snow-heavy fir woods on both sides of the shell-pitted, debris-littered road. Up ahead, mud-splattered U.S. Army vehicles, packed with the survivors of the morning battles, were edging through the village, bumper to bumper. Gigantic siege artillery pieces, jeeps, medium cannon, ammunition carriers, kitchen trucks, laundry vehicles, driven by yellow-eyed Negroes – they all ground painfully slowly towards the west.

Starving Sepp waited till the last Ami half-track, filled with blood-stained infantry, had passed; then he rose from the snowy ditch, chewing a carrot he had found in the field beyond, and waved the torch. Once, twice, three times – the agreed signal.

Cautiously the captured Sherman rolled from the trees and clattered on to the road. The Volkswagen jeep, the two half-tracks and the Tiger followed at carefully worked out intervals.

Von Dodenburg, standing on the turret of the Sherman bare-headed, with his black leather jacket collar turned up to hide his Knight's Cross, gave the hand signal to advance. Slowly the little raiding party began to close up behind the unsuspecting Amis, their tense fingers crooked around the triggers of their weapons, their brows wet with sweat.

'Heaven, arse and twine,' cursed Matz as they swung round a bend and the tumbledown Belgian frontier village came into sight, 'surely the dumb Ami bastards'll spot us soon.'

On the turret, von Dodenburg whispered into the throat mike, 'Stand by Schulze. Matz, we'll swing out of the column just past the church – left. Can you see where I mean?'

'Yes Colonel.'

'Good. We'll nip in there, smartish. The depot is about two hundred metres further in the old village square.'

One by one von Dodenburg's vehicles turned out of the main stream of traffic and headed towards the First Army's POL Depot. The road was deserted save for a smouldering jeep, its rear axle smashed and its dead driver slumped over the steering wheel. As they rolled by it, von Dodenburg saw that someone had looted the dead man's boots, so that even in his death he looked undignified, even foolish.

A sign, bent at a crazy angle and pocked with machine-gun fire, came into sight. 'The depot,' whispered von Dodenburg into the throat mike. 'Round the next bend – stand by every-body!'

Cautiously the Sherman swung round the corner into the old village square. At its far end coloured soldiers were hurrying back and forth, lugging jerricans of gas to the waiting trucks where the drivers were gunning their engines impatiently. Beyond them was a barbed wire enclosure piled four metres high with olive-drab jerricans, and guarded by a couple of obviously scared Negroes armed with a .5 machine gun on a tripod.

'We've got 'em!' von Dodenburg yelled triumphantly, cheered by the sight of so much vital fuel. '*Advance!*'

At the same moment, a concealed American 57 mm anti-tank gun opened up from what looked like a barn. The anti-tank shell struck the Sherman a glancing blow on its steep glacis plate making it rock like a ship at sea. Matz wrenched at the steering rods. Von Dodenburg crashed against the turret and nearly fell out as the one-legged driver flung the Sherman round in a tight turn. At the same time, Schulze flung himself behind the 75 mm. Frantically he pressed the turret motor button. The three men crouched behind the anti-tank gun fired again – and missed. But the 30-ton monster rocked as if it were made of paper and not steel, as the AP[1] shell screeched by it.

'Come on, you shitty asparagus Tarzan,' Matz yelled at Schulze in a frenzy of fear, fighting the controls, 'fire will yer!'

The sweat poured from his big face as Schulze turned the controls frantically. The two triangles met in the sight. He did not dare hesitate another moment. The anti-crew were loading another shell in panicky haste. He pulled the firing lever. The turret filled with acrid smoke. Automatically Schulze opened his mouth to prevent his eardrums from bursting as the shock wave hit him. The breech opened automatically and a steaming yellow shell case clattered to the deck.

As the smoke to the front cleared they heard the grating sound of metal striking metal and the gun disappeared in a ball of ugly yellow and red. Even through the thickness of the Sherman's armour, they could hear the screams of the men they had hit. Then the anti-tank gun lurched to one side, tyre burst, barrel hanging down at an angle like a broken limb.

'Excellent, excellent,' von Dodenburg cried enthusiastically, as machine-gun bullets pattered against the Sherman's sides like rain.

Schulze hadn't time to reply. He sprang to the machine-gun, and the .5 slugs tore into the Negroes at a rate of 500 a minute. A big sergeant tried to bring a bazooka into action. Schulze, the back of his jacket soaked black with sweat, let him have an aimed burst. It cut him in half. Mad or desperate, the SS men never found out, one of the truck drivers, hurled his big two and a half tonner straight at the tank. Schulze fired for the truck's

[1] Armour-piercing shell. (*Transl.*)

windscreen, smashing it immediately and the driver's dark face disappeared behind a spider's web of broken glass.

Five minutes later, it was all over and the handful of survivors were dropping their weapons sullenly at the feet of the victorious panzer grenadiers, who were already asking the 'black apes', as they called them, in broken pidgen English: 'Where your tick-tock, black man?'

Happy, but aware that he had no time to lose if he did not want to snarl up the whole advance to the bridge, von Dodenburg snapped to the panzer grenadier radio operator in the first of the half-tracks: 'You. Send this message to Major Harsch. Tell him – Otto.'

* * *

While they waited for the rest of the Battle Group to catch up with them, Sergeants Matz and Schulze wandered idly through the smashed up depot, but found little to loot in the Negroes' barracks, save a few cigarettes and a couple of cans of Ami 'C' rations, which they tossed away in disgust since most of them seemed to contain lemonade powder.

Matz sniffed: 'That's why they're such shitty soldiers, of course, Schulze. I mean it stands to reason – how can a feller be a soldier, if he drinks lemonade?'

In silence they wandered through the wooden shacks, plastered from wall to ceiling with semi-nude photos of big blondes in black stockings and tight-fitting skirts looking seductively over their bare right shoulders.

'*Grr!*' Schulze bared his teeth and breathed out hard, 'look at the arse on that one – like the backside of a ten dollar horse! By the great whore of Buxtehude, it makes you want to bite holes in the paper.' He gnashed his big teeth together a couple of times to emphasize his point.

Matz pulled a scornful face. 'That's about all yer'll be able to do in this place – that and a visit to the five-fingered widow,' he sniggered and dodged easily as Schulze swung a hamlike fist at him.

But Matz was wrong. As they were about to pass into the next shack, a faint grunt somewhere ahead alarmed them. They brought up their Schmeissers immediately, fingers crooked around the triggers. Cautiously they advanced through the door, prepared to let loose a volley at any moment.

A fat, cheerful looking woman stood in the centre of the room, trying to force black-stockinged hams into a skirt that was much too tight for her. Matz whistled softly and Schulze said in his best French, '*Bonjour Madame, vous jig-jig avec moi?*' he made his intention quite clear with an obscene gesture of his thumb and two fingers.

The woman was alarmed neither by their weapons nor Schulze's proposal. 'Don't talk that lingo to me,' she said in the local German dialect, 'we all speak German here.' With a sigh she let the skirt fall to the floor to reveal tight pink pants. 'I'll never be able to get into that damned skirt!'

'Why bother?' Schulze said, relaxing his hold on his machine-pistol. 'I'd rather see you with it off than on. But what are you doing here anyway?'

The fat woman beamed. She indicated the rumpled bed in the corner of the room. 'Can't you guess, sergeant? You really did give my friend a start.' She shrugged and her huge breasts trembled like puddings under her loose white blouse. 'I hope you didn't hurt the poor lad?'

Matz's bottom lip dropped. 'You don't mean?' He looked at the bed significantly. 'In that – with one of those black apes! Why,' he stuttered, trying to find the right words to express his sense of outrage, 'that ain't . . . proper!'

The woman chuckled hugely. '*Proper*,' she echoed, 'Jesus, Mary, Joseph, I'm the most proper woman alive! In the last five years I have let 'em all have a go at me. French, Belgians, you Germans, the Americans, black and white. They're soldiers, aren't they,' she declared forthrightly, 'whatever their race or nation – just poor lost soldiers, who need a bit of fun, a bit of pleasure.'

'That's right, missus,' Schulze boomed joyfully. 'You tell him – and a lot better than all those lesbian Red Cross wenches with their cups of weak ersatz coffee. It's sex and sympathy the soldier wants – not shitty socks and scarves. Now then, where we gonna do it?'

'Hey, what about me?' Matz protested, waking up suddenly. 'Sod off,' said Schulze busy with his belt buckle.

'But can't we toss for first?' Matz asked, pushing his way forward again.

Without looking behind him, Schulze gave the other NCO a shove in the face which sent him careening against the wall. 'Don't you know by now that rank hath its privileges? I'm the senior NCO, so naturally I get first go – it stands to reason. Now get over to that door and keep your eyes skinned while I get a piece of that lovely grub!' Taking the woman by the hand with affected delicacy, he led her to the rumpled bed which she had just vacated. 'Come, my beloved, let us forget this terrible war in one long pastoral moment.'[1]

* * *

The radio operator doubled across the scuffed snow and snapped to attention in front of Major Harsch.

'Yes?' Harsch barked, taking his eyes from the Jewish-American rabble trembling visibly in the square formed by the half-tracks.

'It's the Colonel, sir. Codeword 'Otto'.'

'Thank you.' He flipped away his cigarette and bellowed, 'Sergeant Ochmann!'

The NCO, his chest stiff with decorations, his right eye covered by a black patch like a pirate, snapped to attention as if he were back at the Sennelager Training Centre. '*Sir!*'

'Mount up. Colonel von Dodenburg has captured Bullingen. We are to follow up immediately. Tanks in the van, the grenadiers bringing up the rear. Better put a Royal Tiger at the point – just in case.'

'Yessir!' Ochmann rapped. 'And the prisoners, sir?'

'What about them?'

Ochmann shrugged slightly, his one eye weighing up the new Major carefully. 'Transport, sir. We can't put them with the grenadiers. They would hinder operations. And we haven't got anything else for them.' He hesitated for just one instant. 'Should we leave them behind?'

[1] A common German phrase for love-making. (*Transl.*)

The suggestion worked, as he knew it would.

'Leave them behind, Ochmann!' Harsch exploded. 'Have you got all your cups in your cupboard, man! If we leave them behind, they could re-arm themselves and attack our rear!'

Harsch bit his lip for a moment. He swung round and stared at the miserable bunch of POWs. What did it matter?, he told himself. Hadn't the Führer himself ordered they should use brutality? Besides who could care in the moment of German victory about the miserable fate of a handful of Americans? He turned back to Ochmann. 'Sergeant,' he said confidentially, 'this is what I want you to do . . .'

* * *

With a roar and clouds of thick blue smoke, half-track after half-track started up. The excited young grenadiers in their mottled camouflaged smocks swung themselves aboard. Behind them the Royal Tigers formed up, intercoms buzzing, the gunners swinging the long hooded 88 mms from side to side easily to test them.

In the centre of the field the miserable American POWs stared at the Germans in bewilderment. 'Say, Mac, what the hell's going on?' asked a beared bareheaded medic of Sergeant Rosenbloom.

The big cook shrugged. 'Who am I – Jesus?'

'Perhaps they're just gonna leave us here,' suggested a wounded MP with a blood-stained bandage around his head, hopefully, as the first half-track started to rattle away in a shower of mud and snow. 'I mean, they just ain't got the wheels to move us—'

His face froze with fear. In the lead half-track, a young panzer grenadier had raised his pistol and began to take aim.

'What the Sam Hill is that guy up to?' cried a Texan voice.

Then the machine-pistols started to chatter. The first vicious burst of lead hissed into their surprised ranks, as a sudden atavistic fury overcame the grenadiers.

'*Stand fast!*' screamed an NCO urgently, hoping to avoid a panic, and fell dead a moment later.

Some of the POWs tried to make a break for it. But they were mown down before they had gone a dozen yards. Others put their hands in front of their eyes as if they wanted to blot out the terrible scene. A few simply waited and accepted their fate stoically. There were wounded and dying men everywhere in the bloody, scuffed snow, and in a few minutes it was all over. For a moment there was silence; then the convoy started to move off with a shot fired here and there whenever a body appeared to twitch. One by one the heavy vehicles lumbered by.

Sergeant Rosenbloom, alive as were perhaps another ten men among the bloody slain prisoners, held his breath. Thank God, they were going! Perhaps he would escape with his life. He waited tensely, his fat dark face wet with sweat and the blood of the dead man next to him. Suddenly he heard the dry throaty crack of a Luger close by, followed by a groan of despair. His heart missed a beat. They were wading through the fallen men looking for those who were not dead.

He held his breath, and raised his head gingerly. A young bareheaded trooper was coming down the line towards him, kicking each corpse systematically. Sergeant Rosenbloom sucked in a great breath of air. A sudden, burning rage overcame him. He was not prepared to be slaughtered like some dumb animal. Cautiously he raised himself. The Kraut was about twenty yards away now. He licked his parched lips. It was now or never. '*Run for it, guys!*' he screamed at the top of his voice, in the hope that there were others still left alive.

He levered himself up and started to pelt across the field. Half a dozen others did the same. A machine-pistol opened up and they scattered wildly. Rosenbloom felt a slug clip him. His heart thumping, his lungs threatening to burst at any moment, he blundered blindly into a clump of trees. He fell and a burst of slugs hissed inches above his head. He was up a second later. '*I must get away . . . I must,*' he gasped in a paroxysm of fear, tears streaming down his unshaven face.

Summoning up the last of his waning strength he staggered into the snowy forest, the only survivor to tell the tale of how Battle Group Wotan had massacred its prisoners.

2

Sunday, December 17th 1944.

It was dawn. Down below on the River Ambleve, the little town of Stavelot lay still, grey and expectant. All the previous day tanks and trucks had rumbled through its ancient winding cobbled streets, bumper to bumper, their decks strewn with sleeping, exhausted GIs, heading west. Occasionally the convoys had been forced to stop for a few moments and the anxious civilians had asked the battle-weary soldiers, 'where are you going? . . . why aren't you staying here to defend us against the Boche?'

The soldiers had avoided looking at them, mumbling something about: 'Don't worry, folks, we're only changing positions – that's all.' And then they had gone, glad to be free of the embarrassing questions and the look of silent reproach in the Belgian civilians' eyes.

Now the town seemed deserted of troops, and its anxious civilians were barricaded in their deep medieval cellars, dug into the side of the steep cliff on which the town was situated, waiting in the candle-flickering icy damp for the attack which must soon come from across the fast-flowing river. But the two shabby civilians, wandering – apparently so aimlessly through the empty cobbled streets – were not so sure that the town was undefended.

And they were right. 'Look Sepp,' Hairless Harry whispered to his skinny companion, 'mg nests.' With a slight nod, he indicated the five machine-guns dug in on both sides of the only bridge across the Ambleve.

Starving Sepp mumbled something, but his twitching nose indicated that, as usual, he had his mind on other things, namely food.

'Can't you think of nothing else but eats?' Harry growled as they walked on up the steep hill from the river.

'Ah, but you don't understand. That's Ami egg and bacon I can smell – lovely eggs and bacon – and where there's such wonderful eats, there's bound to be an HQ.'

Hairless Harry's morose expression did not change – it never did. But he dutifully followed his skinny companion, who was sniffing the cold morning air like some local Ardennes hunting dog following up a strong scent. Five minutes later they found the Ami HQ, a large red-brick house on the top of the cliff, with a dominating view of the whole Ambleve Valley. Cautiously they circled it. Most of its windows were blacked-out with thick khaki U.S. Army blankets. But one or two, curtainless, were open to their prying eyes, and the smell of eggs and bacon led Starving Sepp unerringly to the window of the cookhouse.

Pressing his long red nose against the kitchen window, he stared inside longingly, taking in the sweating cooks, the spluttering frying eggs, the mess assistant shovelling three or four of the golden yellow delicacies on to the waiting men's plates, the mounds of beautiful white bread, the bubbling urns of real coffee. Then he could stand it no longer. With a sigh he took his eyes away from the scene and breathed, 'Harry, it's sheer beauty, sheer beauty! I've never seen anything more wonderful in all my life!'

Hairless Harry, peering in over his shoulder, grunted. All he could see was a noisy, brawling, shoving group of unshaven men, fighting for the eggs, gobbling them down, thick grease dripping down their chins, and jumping up for more.

'I don't call that beautiful,' he said.

Sepp looked at him pityingly. 'Ah, that's because you have no soul, Harry – that's why.'

Harry told him what he could do with his soul; then tried to bring his companion back to reality. Dragging him away from the window, he whispered urgently: 'Now what's the drill?'

'That's obvious,' Sepp answered easily. 'We advise attack.'

* * *

Colonel von Dodenburg frowned thoughtfully at the front-runner. Then picking up his glasses, he peered at the town on the other side of the Ambleve once more. The river itself would present no barrier for his infantry; they could wade it easily. But the bridge, approached at a sixty degree angle, and the narrow streets beyond did create a problem. A couple of determined anti-tank gunners, well emplaced on the other side, could easily hold up his whole Battle Group; then his tanks would have to approach one by one. If one were to be knocked out, it might well block the road completely.

He swung the glasses along the single row of houses, silent yet menacing, which lined the far side of the river. 'You're sure they're empty?' he asked severely.

Sepp nodded confidently. 'There are machine-guns at the bridge – that's all. And further up – that big house you can see – that's the Ami HQ. But they are too busy feeding their faces there to be concerned with fighting.'

Von Dodenburg lowered his glasses and grinned at the front runner. 'That's a strange statement to be coming from you, Sepp,' he said.

'First duty, then food, your Excellency,' Sepp snapped earnestly.

Von Dodenburg sniffed. He did not quite trust the Belgian renegades' information. But he needed that bridge across the Ambleve – and he needed it quick. He looked back at the long line of men and vehicles, hidden beneath the snow-heavy trees which lined the heights overlooking the little town. Some of them would have to die to take it – perhaps die unnecessarily – but that was one of the prices one had to pay for speed and success in war.

Although an inner voice still continued to warn him that the attack on Stavelot might well be a costly business, he knew that he could not waste any more precious time. He must make a decision – now.

'Harsch – Major Harsch.'

'Sir.'

'We attack. Your panzer grenadiers will come in from both flanks, wading the river there – and there.' He indicated the spots he had selected. 'One troop of Tigers will give you covering fire.

'I shall lead the attack on the bridge itself and try to force a way up to the Ami HQ – that red-brick building you can see on the top of the cliff – *there*.'

'I see sir.'

'Your grenadiers and my tanks will rendezvous there – hopefully. Check your watch – it's exactly nine thirty. We attack at zero ten hundred precisely.' He allowed Harsch a moment to adjust his watch, then asked: 'Any questions?'

'Just one, sir. The streets down there appear very confusing. I could do with a guide who knows the lay-out of the place.' He looked significantly at the two shabby front-runners. Colonel von Dodenburg grinned faintly despite his inner tension. 'Why of course, my dear Major! I don't need them this time. You can have them. Indeed they have just assured me that duty is always first.'

'*Merde*,' groaned Hairless Harry angrily and with the side of his boot aimed a vicious kick at Sepp's ankle. 'Now look what kind of shit you've got us into, you damned Walloon chowhound.'

* * *

'What did you say, Colonel?' snapped the Supreme Commander, turning his gaze from the snowflakes falling softly in front of the tall eighteenth century window. Outside in the courtyard there was no sound save the muffled tread of the sentries who had been posted there to guard him ever since the surprise German offensive in the Ardennes had started.

The Provost Colonel knew Ike's rages of old. The newsreels might publicize the Supreme Commander's broad grin and easy 'democratic' manner with his troops; in the privacy of his own HQ, however, he was a different person, touchy, often scowling, and possessed of a very nasty temper.

'I said, sir,' he answered hesitantly, 'that we have a report that the Krauts have been shooting our troops in cold blood in the Ardennes.'

Eisenhower lit another of the sixty *Camels* he chain-smoked a day and exhaled a stream of impatient blue smoke. 'Where – when? Details, Colonel? Facts?'

The portly MP consulted the scrap of paper in his hand, decorated with the West Point class ring. 'One of our patrols picked up a sergeant – a Sergeant Rosenkohl or Rosen*bloom* – can't quite make it out—' Eisenhower clicked his niccotine-stained fingers impatiently and the Colonel hurried on. 'Well, sir, he said he had been captured with a company of infantry, which had been taken by an SS unit. And—'

'Which SS unit?' interrupted Eisenhower once again.

'Wotan – SS Battle Group Wotan, sir.'

'Haven't I heard that name before, Colonel?'

'Yessir,' answered the Provost Colonel, thanking God he had checked up before he had driven across to the Petit Trianon, which was now the Supreme Commander's HQ. 'They gave us a hard time in Italy – at Cassino to be exact, and more recently at Aachen. Elite outfit commanded by an out-and-out Nazi, if our intelligence is correct, named Colonel von Dodenburg.'

Eisenhower nodded.

'Well sir. Without warning and without any provocation, the Krauts started shooting into our men – seems they didn't have the transport to take them with them – and this guy Rosenkohl or – bloom, whatever his name is, was the only survivor. There is no doubt about it,' he hurried on, 'it was an out-and-out, unprovoked, cold-blooded massacre.'

The future President of the United States was a man who could make a decision – a small decision – fast, especially if it were to his advantage. All that long grey morning, with the snow falling outside to remind him unpleasantly that he could not hope for air support for his hard pressed Eight Corps, he had been reading and hearing reports of the breakdown of morale on the Ardennes front, with the green troops up there apparently retreating in their thousands. Might not this be the way to stop the rot, harden their resolve to turn and fight the triumphant enemy?

'Listen,' he said, 'I want that sergeant brought to Supreme Headquarters at once. We'll need his statement for the press. In the meantime I want this story splashed on the front page of the *Stripes*[1] so that the press can pick it up. I'll get Butch[2] to see that it's passed on to the BBC and NBC. We've got to make a big thing of this massacre.'

'Yes, I understand, sir. Anything else, sir?'

'Yeah,' said Eisenhower grimly, 'when this battle is over, I want that guy Dodenburg's head brought to me,' He stabbed out his cigarette in the ash-tray viciously, 'On a goddam silver platter.'

* * *

'Mount up!' yelled Schulze above the roar of the Tigers' motors. 'Come on, you asparagus Tarzans – *move*!'

Behind him the panzer grenadiers seized the extra stick grenades their NCOs were handing out, as if they were free ice-cream cones. Here and there the more nervous of the green-beaks were urinating against the side of the tanks, while the scornful drivers made their usual comment, 'what do you think this is, stubble-hopper – a shitty brothel piss-corner, eh!'

'First tank company, ready!' a harsh NCO's voice reported.

'Second tank company, ready!'

'Third tank company ready – sir!'

Schulze looked up at the CO hanging over the side of the lead Tiger watching the frenzied, noisy preparations for the attack. Stamping his jackboots together, completely ignoring the noise and the blue clouds of diesel coming from the tanks' exhausts, as the drivers gunned their cold engines, he swung von Dodenburg an immaculate salute and yelled at the top of his voice, 'SS Assault Group Wotan ready – *sir*!' But under his voice, he added cynically, 'cannon fodder, ready – for the slaughter.'

'Thank you, Schulze.' Von Dodenburg touched his thin hand casually to his bent, peaked cap. 'All right, mount up yourself.'

Schulze swung himself hastily aboard and dropped into the turret beside the CO. Von Dodenburg spoke into the throat

[1] *The Stars and Stripes*, the US Army newspaper.

[2] Lieutenant Commander Butcher, Eisenhower's public relations aide. (*Transl.*)

mike. Matz crashed home the first of the Tiger's thirty-odd forward gears. Behind it, the rest began to move too, while the panzer grenadiers, tense yet excited at the prospect of their first real action, started to stream down the tree-covered snowy hill-side towards the river below.

Von Dodenburg flung a hasty glance at his watch. Ten exactly. At that moment he heard the hoarse exultant scream of the Battle Group's self-propelled guns as the first salvo struck the far bank. The line of red-brick houses disappeared in a sudden cloud of racing smoke. A second later the electrically-powered six-barrel mortars joined in. Dark, red-tailed rockets hissed through the grey sky, gouging vast holes in the riverbank or hissing into the river, throwing up sparkling silver cascades of water.

Von Dodenburg pulled down the turret hatch. The grenadiers would have to take care of themselves now; the artillery was giving them all the support it could. He had to concentrate on forcing the vital bridge with his Tigers. Thrusting back his peaked cap, he pressed his right eyes to the periscope, while Schulze breathing hard next to him in the green, oily gloom of the turrent, busied himself with the cannon, checking that all systems were released for action and that both HE and AP[1] ammunition were handy for a quick switch-over, in case they bumped into the armour of anti-tank guns.

As they swung round the hill-top bend and the town spread out below them, von Dodenburg pressed both the intercom and radio switches.

'Now get this,' he ordered, 'Lieutenant Simons' tanks and mine will tackle the bridge – the rest of you will hold off. I want no bunching. It would be fatal. If we fail to get the bridge, the next two will try. Over and out!'

Down below Matz changed gear with a savage burst of revs and cursed violently: 'Great crap on the Christmas tree – what has Mrs Matz's boy done to deserve this!'

* * *

The two Tigers, engines roaring in low gears, began slowly to

[1] High explosive and armour-piercing shells. (*Transl.*)

descend the hill towards the silent stone bridge below, their drivers sweating in spite of the cold, as they fought to keep the metal monsters from smashing into each other on the slippery cobbled pavé. On the right, von Dodenburg swung his periscope from side to side, anxiously scanning the bridge. But there was no sign of enemy activity, save the machine-gunners on the other side, crouched behind their ineffectual sandbag screens. At any minute they would spring up in panic, abandon their guns and start racing terror-stricken to the rear. They were nothing to worry about. 'Keep it steady, Simons,' he said evenly. 'Everything's all right.'

'Yessir,' the eighteen-year-old lieutenant's voice came crackling back, but there was no mistaking the tension in it. Lieutenant Simons was going into action for the first time.

The first slugs from the Ami machine-gunners began to patter harmlessly off the Tiger's thick sides. Von Dodenburg swung the periscope round.

'Shall I tickle 'em up, sir?' queried Schulze, grabbing the machine-gun handle.

Von Dodenburg shook his head. 'No, they'll be making dust in a minute. Don't waste ammo on them.'

The bridge was getting closer and closer now. Von Dodenburg could make out every detail and beyond it the cluster of little shops: a barber's with its silver hanging plate, a newsagent's with the *La Meuse* signs still outside, a *bistro*, its window decorated with *Stella Artois* signs. He began to relax. They would take the bridge without trouble after all.

He pressed the throat mike. 'All right, Schulze, you might as well give those wet tails on the machine-gun—'

He stopped short. A brilliant light blinked beyond the *bistro*. A wild tearing noise struck the air – he could hear it even above the roar of the Tiger's engine. The Tiger rocked violently like a ship in a storm and a shower of debris pattered down on to the turret. He ducked instinctively, momentarily deafened. He swung the periscope round, and gasped at what he saw.

Simons' Tiger had been struck by the anti-tank shell! One track lay across the road in front of it. White smoke was pouring furiously from the engine.

'Simons!' he called excitedly, 'Bail out man – *bail out!*'

No reply from the stricken tank.

'*Simons!*'

The zinc-like light flashed again. They heard a roaring hush like an express train hurtling by. The Tiger swung back and forth, with Matz madly fighting the controls, trying to prevent the 60-ton monster from overturning.

'Anti-tank!' he screamed furiously. 'Beyond the boozer!'

'*At three o'clock,*' yelled Schulze.

Von Dodenburg forgot Simons. 'Advance and make smoke – quick!'

Without waiting for Matz, he pressed the smoke discharge trigger. Three lazy black cannisters spun into the air. For a moment nothing happened. The white tracer continued to scud off their cupola like crazy golf balls. Then one after another the three smoke grenades exploded and thick white smoke billowed up in front of them.

Schulze snatched the firing bar back blindly. The great tank shuddered. The 88 mm shell shot wildly up the street, smashing harmlessly into a church, way beyond the cunningly sited Ami anti-tank gun. Stone and rubble showered down on the turret, but as the artificial fog in front of them grew thicker, a suddenly worried von Dodenburg realized that the anti-tank gun was still in position and that Battle Group Wotan had a fight on its hands.

* * *

The panzer grenadiers, the elite of the nation, began to wade confidently into the water. Beyond them the smoke-shrouded row of brick houses lining the opposite bank of the river were silent. If they had once contained any Amis, they told themselves, the initial barrage must have sent them scurrying for better cover or killed them where they stood.

Harsch, pistol in hand, peaked cap set jauntily on the side of his head, paused in mid-stream, the racing water tearing at his elegantly booted legs, 'Keep spread out,' he ordered above the noise of the battle at the bridge. 'Sergeant Ochmann – keep them spread out!'

They were only a matter of metres from the other side. Starving Sepp, sucking a pebble he had picked up on the riv-erbed, felt they might make it. 'Harry,' he said, 'when we make it, up that street on the left sharp. That's the quickest way to the eats!'

And that was when the first high-pitched, hysterical burst of enemy machine-gun fire ripped into the front rank of the grena-diers struggling through the fast-running shallows.

Harsch blew his whistle shrilly. 'Forward!' he yelled. 'At the double!'

The grenadiers, aware that they were sitting ducks as long as they remained in the water, struggled forward, firing from the hip in wild bursts as they waded desperately for the far bank. Then the whole line of smoke-shrouded houses along it erupted into fire. Red tracer screamed towards the Germans. Men fell everywhere, but the grenadiers pressed on, stumbling over their dead and dying comrades lying thrashing in the bloody shal-lows. Ochmann, the veteran of five years of war, flung himself panting into a mud hole and start to dig frantically with his entrenching tool just as a grenade exploded with a vivid flash above his head. Yet the fanatical young men of Wotan pressed on with Major Harsch at their head until at last they were in the houses. Crashing through the sagging doors, diving through the shattered windows, the young men went wild. A rifle butt to an Ami's face. The Ami staggering back, as if he had suddenly run into a brick wall. A boot to a corporal's crotch. His scream stiffled by hot vomit. Frantic fingers grabbing for ruined geni-tals. A burst to the face and sudden blood-filled holes where the eyes had been. A spade slice to the stomach. The Ami on his knees trying to staunch the gaping wound.

But when the slaughter was over and the first row of houses were firmly in their hands, a panting, blood-stained, hatless Major Harsch saw that he was trapped. Already heavy artillery shells – coming from a long way away – were beginning to fall in the river behind him, while ahead new Amis had taken pos-session of a tall eighteenth century factory which barred his way up the cliff. Wearily he turned to his exhausted young men, swaying on their feet, their eyes wild with shock.

'We're cut off,' he gasped. 'Start . . . start to dig in . . . Prepare for a counter-attack . . .'

The panzer grenadier attack had failed.

* * *

Colonel von Dodenburg clubbed his fist down on the 88 mm's massive breech block angrily. 'The damn, damn fool!' he cursed, 'couldn't he have expected the Amis would be waiting for him in those damn houses!'

Schulze squatting next to him in the green gloom of the turret, listening to the regular hollow thump of the Ami anti-tank gun which still had them trapped at the bridge, said nothing. His private opinion of Major Harsch would be better kept to himself; he did not want a quick trip to Torgau[1] for insolence to an officer.

He waited till the CO had worked off his rage at the new report, then ventured: 'Sir, I don't think we're going to do it with the Tiger – those Amis out there have got us by the short and curlies, that's for shitty sure.'

Von Dodenburg knew that Schulze was right. Once the Tiger ventured on to the bridge again, it would soon suffer Simons' fate. The American anti-tank gun crew would brew him up and every tank that followed him too, until their ammunition or courage ran out. Before they retreated, they would blow up the little stone bridge across the Ambleve and Wotan's advance would be stopped for good; there was no other way of crossing the river for his heavier tanks. They would be stuck on the heights until the Ami dive-bombers found a hole in the cloud cover and came roaring in on them to blast them out of existence.

The worried young Colonel nodded slowly. 'What do you suggest we do, Schulze?'

'Well, sir, it stands to reason that we're not going to do it in this particular sledge,' he rapped the wall of the turret with his hamlike fists. 'So, sir, my belief is that we'll have to tackle that gun on foot.'

[1] Notorious military prison. (*Transl.*)

'I agree, but that shitty gun is covered by the Ami mg nest in the *pissoir*, beyond the newspaper shop!'

'And a very proper place for it to be,' sniffed Schulze. 'But I know what you mean, sir. Before we could have a go at the anti-tank gun, those shits in the *pissoir* would see us off sharpish. So we've got to cover our approach.'

'How?'

'Use a tank to put out the mg crew while we tackle the anti-tank gun, coming under the bridge instead of over it or through the water.'

Von Dodenburg's keen blue eyes lit up; then the light died away. 'But who can I ask to volunteer for that kind of Ascension Day[1] mission, Schulze? It's be a one-way ticket to heaven!'

Schulze grinned triumphantly at his CO. 'We'll leave that problem to our technical genius below us.' He kicked Matz's shoulder playfully.

'Hey, give over,' objected Matz sharply. 'Who the hell are you, you Hamburg wet-tail, to volunteer Mrs Matz's son for an Ascension Day mission?'

'Don't wet yer frilly knickers,' Schulze answered lightly. 'You won't get hurt – unless you make a mess of things and I have to give you a taste of the old Hamburg equalizer,' (he meant his brass knuckles) 'to learn you a little bit of respect for a senior NCO. This is how we're gonna do it . . .'

* * *

Just after one it started to snow at Stavelot. The grey sky turned a menacing leaden colour and then without warning, unleashed a bitter white fury on the struggling mortals below. The men grouped around the anit-tank gun were virtually blinded, their vision limited to a matter of yards.

The gun-commander huddled deeper into his long slicker and ordered grimly: 'Stand by, fellers! Sure as hell, they're gonna use this crap to cover another attack!'

Obediently the three-man crew crouched around the slim, long-barrelled anti-tank gun, surrounded by gleaming yellow

[1] Military expression for an impossible task. (*Transl.*)

shell-cases, already being covered by the fury of the sudden snow storm, while their sergeant peered over the edge of the shield, trying to make out the bridge.

Across the road, sprawled out on the stinking, tiled floor of the metal-walled *pissoir*, the frozen machine-gun crew did the same, peering out underneath the wall at the swirling whiteness. Suddenly the anti-tank sergeant tensed. He thought he had heard something. He turned his head to one side, ignoring the icy snow flakes slipping down his collar, straining to identify the sound. For a moment he told himself he was imagining it. Then he knew he wasn't. It was the clatter of tank tracks all right, muted by the thick wall of snow admittedly. But there – definitely there.

'Here they come,' he gasped. 'Check yer round, Shorty – quick!'

Swiftly and expertly, the gun-layer's assistant whipped the breech-handle back. 'Okay, sarge,' he said, the tension obvious in his voice.

'Good. Dude, keep her at two o'clock. Even if you can't see the Kraut bastard, you'll hear him okay. When I tell you to fire, no shitting – *fire*. Okay?'

'Yes sarge,' answered Dude, the 304 Anti-Tank Company's snappiest dresser and crack shot. 'Wilco.'

'Kay, stand by, everybody, here the bastards come. And I hope to hell that those Joes over there in the pisshouse are keeping their peepers skinned for Heini infantry.'

The Sergeant tensed as the clatter of tank tracks grew louder, his frozen hand raised just above the gun-layer's shoulder. Across the white-covered cobbled street, the two man mg crew waited expectantly too for the infantry which would cover the enemy tank. The gunner's finger crooked slowly around his trigger, his right eye narrowed against the howling snow storm. One more second . . . one more . . .

The Tiger, its gun protruding before it, loomed up suddenly out of the driving snow. The sergeant slapped his hand down on the gun-layer's shoulder hard. The Dude pressed his right eye against the rubber eye-piece of the sight and jerked the lever back. The lean gun erupted, its braked wheels lifting from the snow-covered cobbles. A 57mm shell cracked flatly towards the buttoned-down monster.

'Dead on!' the sergeant screamed, as the big Tiger reeled violently.

'*Load!*' yelled Dude, as the steaming yellow shell case clattered to the ground.

The loader thrust home a new shell. The breech lever snapped upwards and Dude frantically adjusted the sights. On the bridge the Tiger had righted itself. It careened forwards blindly, smashing against the the side of the bridge and moving off angle.

In the *pissoir*, the machine-gun opened up and the two-man crew poured a vicious stream of tracer at the Tiger's turret. If the Krauts tried to bale out now, they would be mown down without mercy.

'*Fire!*' the anti-tank sergeant yelled.

Dude jerked back the firing bar. Again the gun erupted. At that range he couldn't miss. The shell hissed through the driving snow and the Tiger reared up on its hind sprockets like a bucking bronco, heeling back and forth, yet still it came on with the white smoke pouring from its turret, thicker and thicker by the second.

'Christ on a crutch!' the anti-tank sergeant screamed. 'Why don't the Heini bastards bale out—' His words ended in a gasp of horror as he saw that the stricken Tiger, now completely out of control, was heading straight for the two men crouched on the floor of the *pissoir*. '*Run for it,*' he bellowed, cupping his hand to his mouth, '*RUN—*'

A rending crash drowned his words. The Tiger rammed into the *pissoir*. What had once been a man became a pressed out bag of crushed bones and bloody pulp on the wall, as the stricken Tiger came to a final rest. Then the Tiger's fuel tanks exploded and the remains of the *pissoir* became a huge funeral pyre of oily, scarlet flame.

'Oh, my holy Christ,' gasped the sergeant, 'the poor unlucky bastards!'

It was then that von Dodenburg and Schulze, chests heaving with the effort, emerged from beneath the bridge. For a moment they stood there in the whirling snow, silhouetted against the fierce crackling red. Then von Dodenburg brought up the one-shot *Panzerfaust* and almost without aiming, jerked back the trigger.

'Sarge – look out!' Dude screamed frantically in warning. *'Sarge!'*

The projectile exploded with a roar on the wall above them. and the sergeant crumpled to the ground. Schulze pushed the CO aside, aimed and fired. The slow projectile, packed with high explosive, struck the gun. Dude was flung into the air, without his legs. The gun-loader was slammed against the wall, before the gun itself disintegrated in an ear-splitting roar.

* * *

Von Dodenburg's face was still black from the explosion of the Panzerfaust grenade as he walked slowly through the basement of the captured U.S. Headquarters, packed now with their own wounded. Most of the young panzer grenadiers wounded in the river crossing, lay on the icy stone floors, still clad in their filthy, bloody uniforms, covered with dirty overcoats, sacking, looted Ami blankets – anything the hard-pressed orderlies could find.

Von Dodenburg's eyes filled with tears. He remembered them marching in to join the Battle Group a mere month before; now they were dying on the floor of some damn Belgian office block.

Impulsively he bent down and stroked a dying boy's sweat-damp brow, smoothing back his matted blond hair. 'Well done,' he said softly. 'You have done very well.' Then he looked round at the crowded improvised ward and clicking his heels together, he brought his dirty hand to the rim of his cap. 'German soldiers, men of Wotan, *comrades*, I salute you!'

His officers were waiting for him in the hastily evacuated Ami map room, and they looked at him expectantly as he entered. But he spoke first to Schulze: 'Have the radio men made any contact? Sixth Army HQ? The Reich Division? Anybody?'

Schulze shook his head. 'No sir. Not a sausage. We haven't been able to raise nothing.'

'It's the hills, sir,' Matz said, still pleased with the way he had managed to jam the lone Tiger's accelerator with his wooden leg, although he was now hobbling around with the aid of a captured Ami rifle. 'They cut down our range drastically.'

Von Dodenburg nodded. 'I suppose so. All right, gentlemen, can I have your attention?' He swept the littered table clear of obstructions and spread out his map, anchoring it in place with the white-hissing Coleman gasoline lamp and an American 38 grenade. 'This is the position, gentlemen. Our grenadiers have taken serious losses today, as you know. Major Harsch here reports twenty per cent casualties. Fortunately our tank losses have been exceedingly light – two Tigers. So, we have the punch, but very little with which to follow that punch up. Nevertheless, it is our task to capture that bridge tomorrow. We shall leave the problem of follow-up to the Butcher Boy.'

There was a cackle of weary laughter from the dirty, worn young officers.

'Now, this is my plan. At first light we shall move out. Tanks in the lead, Harsch's grenadiers in the rear. I want to husband the infantry from now onwards – we shall need them on the ground once we've got the bridge.' He pointed a dirty forefinger at the cracked map with its smeared overlay. 'We shall take the Trois Ponts road here, then swing westwards to Werbomont. As far as that, the road and the terrain will be perfectly lousy. Fortunately Intelligence says that we won't meet with much in the way of opposition, a few engineers, base troops, civil affairs people and the like. Once we clear Werbomont, we shall reach the exit out of these damned Ardennes hills. We will be on the main motor-road to Huy. Thereafter, it should be plain sailing – I hope.' He paused. 'Any questions?'

'What about this place – Stavelot, sir?' asked Deschner, CO of the Second Tank Company.

Von Dodenburg knew that the young officer was worried about the future of the wounded packed in the cellars below. But he knew he had to be hard. Everything had to be sacrificed to the capture of the bridge.

'We have no men to spare to defend it. I need all available infantry up front. Doctor Dietz will remain behind with the gravely wounded. The rest will be re-armed and either continue with ourselves, or stay here and defend their wounded comrades.'

'But sir, you know full well what will happen to our wounded if the Amis retake this place,' Deschner said hotly, flashing a significant look at Harsch, 'after what the Major did yesterday to those Ami POWs?'

Von Dodenburg looked at him in bewilderment. 'What in three devils' name, do you mean, Deschner?'

But before the embarrassed young officer could answer, a harassed radio operator came into the room, clicked his heels together at the door and snapped: 'Blitz[1] from General Dietrich, sir.'

Schulze snatched the message from his hand. 'Sod off, you horrible herald of doom, you,' he hissed out of the side of his mouth and passed the message to the young CO.

Von Dodenburg ran his eye across it swiftly and then looked at the expectant officers. 'Gentlemen, the Butch-Boy informs us that the Sixth Army's situation, as of fourteen hundred hours, is as follows: "THE REICH STALLED. ENEMY COUNTER-ATTACKING LOSEHEIM GAP LOCALLY. THIRD PARA AND 265TH PEOPLES GRENADIER BOGGED DOWN. REPORT POSITION IMMEDIATELY. DIETRICH." ' Contemptuously he let the flimsy slip of paper fall to the floor. 'You understand what that message means, don't you?'

No one answered, but their grim worn faces told they had comprehended its import well enough.

He nodded slowly. 'We are cut off, gentlemen – at least temporarily. Now we must go it alone.'

[1] Urgent communication. (*Transl.*)

3

Monday, December 18th 1944.

'Okay, gentlemen, the time has come for us to stop pussy-footing around,' the usually courteous General Courtney Hodges, commander of the U.S. First Army, glared at his staff assembled in the map room of Spa's Hotel Britannica. 'It's either root-hog or die! From here on in, we've got to shoot the works, do you understand?'

His staff did. They could hear the faint rumble of the guns from the direction of Trois Ponts, and down below the panicked rear-echelon 'canteen commandos' were already throwing their personal gear into the waiting trucks, continually glancing over their shoulders as if they expected the Kraut panzers to come barrelling down the steep hill that led into the little Belgian resort town. It wouldn't be long before they had to abandon their HQ. Already the long, pathetic lines of shabby civilian refugees were beginning to file past the hotel's mock Gothic façade.

'You all know the mess Eighth Corps had gotten itself into at the front. Now the Huns seems to be everywhere. So I want everybody in this Army to understand we are not going to fight this battle in a half-cocked manner.' Hodges, the ex-infantryman who had fought the Germans in the old war, looked round the faces of his staff grimly. 'If those Hun sons-of-bitches want war in the raw, then we're going to give it to them. First priority, stop this armoured drive, led by that killer Colonel von—' he clicked his fingers in irritation, 'What's the guy's damned name?'

'Von Dodenburg, sir,' said an immaculate aide hurriedly. 'Colonel von Dodenburg.'

'Yes, that's the bastard. I want him stopped and I want him stopped today! Now it's pretty obvious what the Kraut's after – a way out of the Ambleve valley so that he can get some mileage out of those darned Tigers of his. The problem is – which way? There are two routes open to him if he wants to reach the Meuse – which he obviously does. Through Werbomont or here through Spa. My guess is Spa. But gentlemen, I'm not going to take any chances. I want von Dodenburg stopped at Trois Ponts. Throw in everybody you've got – canteen commandos, clerks, cooks, MPs. Anybody who can goddam walk and carry a rifle, do you understand?' He crashed his fist down on the table angrily.

At that moment there was a knock at the door. Colonel Dickson, Hodges' elderly Chief-of-Intelligence hurried in. He was visibly shaken. Ignoring the rest of the brass assembled in the big room, he said: 'General, if you don't want to get captured, you'd better get out of town. The Germans are only a mile away.'

Hodges raised a hand. 'Now, now, Monk, you're going to be my strategic reserve.'

'But General, I insist!' said Dickson urgently. 'One of our scout planes managed to get below the cloud. They're heading this way for sure.'

Hodges considered for a moment. 'Okay. We'll move back. But remember this, gentlemen, I want that Kraut bastard von Dodenburg *stopped*!'

Minutes later the man who commanded an army 300,000 strong strode through the big salon, where a quarter of a century before Kaiser William the Second had recognized his defeat and abdicated, and entered the big olive-drab auto, whose nervous driver was already gunning his engine. The driver crashed home first and drove off quickly westwards. First Army's HQ had been abandoned. Spa lay open for the taking.

* * *

A dark figure loomed up out of the swirling snow, hand upraised with an order to stop. Behind him Sergeant Rosenbloom could make out an improvised road barrier, manned by grim-faced MPs, clutching grease-guns. The driver from Supreme Headquarters tapped the jeep's brakes gingerly and the snow-covered vehicle came to an awkward halt.

The big police lieutenant shoved an extended hand towards him. 'Papers,' he demanded.

Rosenbloom noted that he kept his other hand clutched on his forty-five. The snow was falling in great heavy flakes now as if it would never stop.

The MP examined the papers '*Who's Babe Ruth?*' he suddenly shot at the HQ's driver.

He groaned. 'Aw, fer Chrissake, Lieutenant! Not that again! All the way from Malmedy, some Joe or other has been stopping me and asking me who the hell Babe Ruth is – or who's Betty Grable's goddam husband?'

The MP nodded, but he did not return their travel authorization. 'Okay,' he snapped, 'drive your vehicle off on to the verge there and pull your rifles.'

The driver looked up at the officer's snow-wet face, as if he had suddenly gone crazy. 'What did you say – pull rifles? I've got to get the sarge here back to Versailles to Supreme HQ. Ike wants him personally.'

'I don't care if the goddam Pope wants him! My orders are to grab every goddam body I can see and put 'em into a composite rifle company. You're a body, soldier, so haul ass.'

A protest died on the jeep driver's lips, as the MP's hand clenched threateningly on the butt of his forty-five. 'Okay . . . okay, I'm coming,' he said resignedly.

Five minutes later Sergeant Rosenbloom, the one-time short order cook, found himself, rifle over his shoulder, in the infantry, ploughing his way through the thick, snow-bound pine forest towards the River Ambleve and the narrow winding road that led from Trois Ponts to Spa.

* * *

The going was murderous. The snow swept in in thick bitter flurries, blinding the purple-faced lookouts and tank commanders, as they stood huddled on the Tigers' turrets peering through the white gloom for the first sign of the enemy.

Wotan was leaving Trois Ponts, heading for the turn-off through the narrow Ambleve valley towards Werbomont. Frequently a tank would skid wildly and go careening towards one of the ditches that bound the road on both sides, its sweating, cursing driver desperately fighting the controls. Sometimes a tank would hover on the edge of the ditch, see-sawing back and forth before crashing over in a thick flurry of snow; whirling, useless tracks; roaring, impotent motors. Then the engineers, aided by grenadiers, would have to rush forward and begin the back-breaking, time-consuming task of getting it out. But mostly the inexperienced drivers managed to keep the metal monsters on a road often worse than a skating rink, fighting every metre of the treacherous going.

Colonel von Dodenburg huddled up in a captured U.S. greatcoat, in the lead tank, was thankful for the snow storm, for it gave him cover from Ami air attack. On the narrow valley road, hemmed in on one side by a steep hillside and on the other by the Ambleve, he knew he wouldn't have a chance in hell if the Ami fighter-bombers caught him. Now the only danger to his attempt to break out of the Ardennes at Werbomont would come from the ground.

He pressed his throat-mike. 'Listen flak. Stand down air watch. There'll be no air attack in this weather. Prepare to use your guns in a ground role. Over and out.'

Further back in the column, the three lumbering half-tracks, armed with four quick-firing 20 mm anti-aircraft guns, swung their guns down and directed them to the left, facing the river while the long, well-spaced column rattled on. In the lead Tiger, Schulze, who had taken over from Matz as driver, thrust the tank into the ever-deepening snow on the empty road in front of them as if it were a snowplough, the Tiger's engine howling in protest at the strain. Time passed leadenly and still there was no sign of the turn-off to Werbomont where a narrow road bridge crossed the Ambleve. Von Dodenburg began to peer at his wrist-watch anxiously.

It was just after two, with the snow still beating down on them furiously, that the first flare hissed into the steaming white sky on the other side of the Ambleve and hung there, bathing the snow below a garish blood-red for a moment, before plunging into the water.

'Amis!' grunted Matz, crouched over the gun next to von Dodenburg.

Von Dodenburg nodded grimly. 'I'm afraid so.'

Matz laughed scornfully. 'Don't worry, sir. They can't fight their way out of a paper bag – a *wet* paper bag. Why, one fart from old Schulze down there, especially after one of those pea-soups the kitchen bulls make, and half of them would keel over.'

As von Dodenburg forced a smile, Schulze's indignant voice came crackling over the intercom: 'I heard that, you short-assed cripple! And one burst of arse flak from you, with the kind of green smoke you give out, and the lot of 'em would turn up their toes and start looking at the shitty potatoes from below.'

The convoy rumbled on. But now it was accompanied by a series of flares, red, white and green. At regular intervals they shot into the air to illuminate the SS men's tense young faces in their garish light before the snow or water extinguished them, in a sudden hush.

'What the goddam hell are those Amis over there playing at,' Matz snarled angrily as yet another flare exploded only fifty metres in front of the crawling Tiger, 'shitty cowboys and Indians!'

'Shut up!' ordered Colonel von Dodenburg harshly. 'Look!'

'What sir?'

'The turn-off to Werbomont!'

In front of them, a gap had appeared suddenly in the driving snow to reveal the crazily-tilted sign for Werbomont and beyond it a fragile, narrow bridge over the river. Von Dodenburg pressed the throat mike hastily.

'Bear right, Schulze.'

'Already seen it, sir,' Schulze answered. 'Just preparing for a nice little *pas de deux* across to the left. This snow's like shitty glass! Stand by in the turret. Here we go – and if we land in the river, don't forget to bury me with full military honours.'

As Schulze started to edge gingerly to the left, pulling the left steering rod, braking and releasing it instantly as soon as the track appeared to skid, von Dodenburg knew what he meant. If the Tiger went over the bank into the river, he wouldn't have a chance. Millimetre by millimetre, his big hands wet with sweat, the ex-docker guided the 60-tonner across the road towards the bridge. Behind him the rest of the convoy had rolled to a halt. With bated breath the crews watched Schulze approach the bridge.

Twice he braked too hard. Twice the tank skidded towards disaster, angry red sparks rising from its tracks. Twice the watchers gasped with horror, as the Tiger headed for the bank apparently out of control; and twice a sweating, cursing Schulze managed to catch it just in time.

Millimetre by millimetre the far edge of the little stone bridge came forwards to meet them. There was no danger from the bank now, but von Dodenburg, leaning far out of the snow-encrusted turret and shouting urgent instructions to Schulze, knew that if the driver miscalculated, the Tiger could block the whole bridge. Then Schulze did it, with one final roar of the tank's protesting engine. And as he did so, the Ami attack hit the stalled convoy.

To their left from the other side of the river a lone machine-gun began to chatter slowly from the cover of the fir forest there.

'Get those tanks over the river,' von Dodenburg yelled urgently over the radio. 'Panzer grenadiers – take up defensive positions. Drivers get your guns round. *Fire!*'

But as the panzer grenadiers dropped stiffly over the sides of their half-tracks and stumped towards the ditch lining the river bank, there was no answering crack from the Tiger's 88s. Von Dodenburg now realized that the road was too narrow for the gunners to bring their turrets round without crashing the long-barrelled weapons into their neighbours.

'For Christ's sake,' he screamed. 'Get that flak into action!'

Khaki-clad figures were emerging from the woods, running clumsily across the thick snow towards the trapped panzers. Shouting hoarsely in triumph, they were only a hundred metres away, hundreds of them. But their sense of triumph at having trapped the tanks on the bridge was short-lived for a second later the thin-barrelled flak cannons started to thump their music of death.

Men dropped everywhere in the snow. Screaming, groaning, cursing, moaning. Clapping hands to ruined faces, shattered knees, holed chests, ripped guts, the first wave disappeared in seconds. Behind them the officers of the second wave blew shrill, urgent whistles. A new group broke raggedly from the trees. Again the sweating flak gunners opened up with their terrible weapons, tearing great gaps in the Amis' ranks, until they were only fifty metres away, and at last they broke, fleeing, bowling over their comrades, stamping on the wounded, throwing away their weapons.

They came once more. Cautiously this time, trying to outflank the flak guns from the right rear. It was the opportunity for which the nervous Tiger gunners at the end of the column had been waiting. The thunderous roar reverberated through the tight confines of the narrow valley as they brought their great 88s into action.

* * *

Shells were screaming down on the ragged lines of the composite companies in a continuous, ear-splitting roar, throwing up huge brown and white holes ahead of them. Still the ex-cooks, clerks, drivers, Army Air Corps men advanced, chivvied and threatened by the combat-experienced officers and NCOs who led them.

'Awright, keep moving, you guys,' yelled Rosenbloom's NCO, a bandy-legged, ugly master-sergeant whom everybody called 'VD'. 'You've had it if you stop! Besides them goddam Krauts are still using AP . . . They must be rookies! Come on now, keep moving . . .'

The line advanced hesitantly towards the rear of the long German column on the other side of the river. Here and there a man dropped with a sudden groan or a frantic cry of 'medic'. But the Noncoms tolerated no stopping, even for the wounded. The earth rose up and shook. Trees splintered. Their branches tumbled to the snow, leaving them white and broken. Still VD urged them on, with his persistent rasped: 'Keep moving . . . keep moving!'

They were nearly at the river when the Tiger gunners tumbled to the fact they were using the wrong ammunition. There was a moment's pause in the barrage and the GIs broke into a heavy, clumsy run, their packs flopping up and down on their khaki-clad backs.

'That's it, fellers,' VD cried enthusiastically. 'We've nearly got 'em by the short and curlies now.'

Crack! Directly above Rosenbloom a shell burst with a dry hoarse frighteningly new sound.

'*Air bursts!*' screamed VD, as men fell everywhere.

The steam went out of the American attack. The survivors broke, throwing away their weapons in their haste to get away from that terrible fire. 'Come back – for Chrissake – *come back!*' VD yelled at them furiously. He levelled his pistol and prepared to fire at their defenceless backs. A panic-stricken helmetless soldier blundered into him blindly and set him reeling to one side. Another salvo of air bursts descended upon the few who stood their ground, motionless and somehow foolish as they hesitated there.

'All right, guys,' yelled VD above the screams of the new wounded. 'Let's get the goddam hell outa here!'

They needed no urging. As the full weight of the German barrage exploded above them like the final fury of some great storm, they turned and doubled back the way they had come.

'Hellfire,' Sergeant Rosenbloom panted as he ran with the rest, 'will nothing stop the Kraut bastards?'

* * *

'What did you goddam say?' Hodges exploded, standing beside his staff car on the narrow road, the snow falling on his shoulders unheeded.

The red-faced Captain who had brought the bad news hesitated; it wasn't every day that a junior confronted his Army Commander with the information that his soldiers had fled from the field of battle.

'Well, get on with it, Captain!' Behind Hodges the whole staff column was stalled, waiting impatiently to get on to the new HQ.

'Sir, the attack regiment broke and ran.'

Hodges looked at the captain aghast.

'But sir,' the captain hurried on, 'they took terrific casualties. Out there, the fields are covered with their dead. And besides,' he added desperately, 'Most of them weren't infantry, just cooks and clerks, who—'

'I don't care if they were latrine sweepers,' Hodges interrupted brutally, 'they were American soldiers ... American doughs who broke and ran. Get me the Ninth Tac,' he snapped to an aide. 'I want to talk to those fly boys.'

A few moments later General Hodges was crouched in the radio half track talking to General Van Damn of the 9th TAC. 'Joe, I want those Krauts taken out and I want them taken out *now*!'

'But General,' protested the Air Force Commander. 'I don't know what the weather's like where you are, but it's hell here. My boys have been socked in all day.'

'I don't know about that, Joe. That's your problem. Find a hole in the cloud – anything, but take those Krauts out for me – and goddam quick.'

'But sir, it isn't as easy as that. My boys—'

'Your *boys*,' Hodges interrupted harshly, 'better get their asses into their planes while there's still any light left or there'll be one Army Air Corps general officer less in the ETO[1]. You read me?'

Thirty minutes later the six twin-engined Mitchells and nine Mustangs of the 322nd Bombardment Group were airborne, and flying in a gleaming silver V towards the Ambleve valley, while their pilots scanned the billowing thick grey clouds below for the break they had to find. The hunt for von Dodenburg's panzers was on.

* * *

Despite the conditions, the convoy's pace had picked up. With a couple of Harsch's half-tracks, packed with confident if frozen young grenadiers in the lead in case the Amis tried to ambush them again, the long column rolled up the road towards

[1] European Theater of Operations. (*Transl.*)

the key town of Werbomont at a good fifteen kilometres an hour. In the packed Volkswagen jeep, Matz and the two Belgian front-runners snored in the back seat, while von Dodenburg sitting next to Schulze, the driver, prepared his attack on Werbomont. Assuming that the Amis would have realized by now what his objective was – Werbomont and the Meuse bridge – he anticipated trouble at Werbomont, but nothing serious. The massacre at the bridge outside Trois Ponts had proved the Ami generals were throwing in the scrapings of the barrel – raw, inexperienced levies, who had about as much idea of an infantry attack as he had of the moon. Now nothing could stop them reaching their objective. Folding up his map, he relaxed as best he could in the icy jeep and stared contentedly at the snowy fields racing by.

'Everything all right, sir?' Schulze inquired, not taking his eyes off the half-track only ten metres in front of him, its wheels churning up flurries of snow which he fought to beat from his windscreen with the poorly functioning wipers.

'As you would say,' his CO answered, 'everything's in butter.'

'Let's say in margarine, sir.'

Von Dodenburg gave him a sharp look. 'What's that supposed to mean, Schulze?'

'Not much, sir. But I don't think I'd take any bets that I'll be tucked up in some plump whore's nice warm bed in Antwerp in a couple of days' time, getting some nice juicy oats.'

Von Dodenburg looked at the big Hamburger who had fought at his side for five long years now. 'You don't think we'll pull it off then, Schulze?'

'We might make the bridge, sir – that I'll grant you.' He hit the brake momentarily and then released his foot the next instand. '*Christ on a crutch* – that half-track driver shouldn't be allowed to drive a pram!' he cursed, 'but I think that'll be it. Even if the Butcher Boy has the strength to get to Antwerp, he doesn't have the fuel – as everybody in the Group knows. What then? We'll be stuck at the bridge, hoping the stubble-hoppers will catch up with us. And even if they do, how are they going to shittingly well continue from there?'

'Let that be the Butcher Boy's worry. Our objective is the bridge. Let's get to Huy first.'

'As you say, sir,' Schulze said and, concentrating on his driving, relapsed into a gloomy silence.

More kilometres passed. Once they ran into a group of Ami stragglers. There was ragged little fire fight. But Harsch's grenadiers scattered them without too much difficulty and the GIs fled back into the snowy fir forest from which they had come. Once von Dodenburg thought he heard the faint drone of aircraft. In sudden alarm he scanned the grey sky. But there was nothing in sight, and he dismissed the sound as a product of his imagination. Nothing could fly in this weather. Besides in half an hour it would be dark and then they would be completely safe against air attack. Closing his eyes, he began slowly to sink into sleep – his first in the last forty-eight hours.

* * *

'In all my goddam life, I've never felt as cold as this,' said the Southerner, squatting in the snow, shivering, his face violet. 'Goddam, it seems to freeze the nuts right off'n ya.'

'Yer get your share of it, buddy,' replied the little bandy-legged sergeant they called VD. He yawned with the icy cold and set the whole little group of survivors crouched in the firs yawning. It was the only sound now, save for the soft sighing of the wind and periodic soft slithering of the snow it blew from the branches of the trees.

Rosenbloom, shivering violently, his ashen face buried deep inside the collar of his greatcoat which seemed, for some reason, to smell of horse manure, looked at the little Noncom, and wondered why he'd gotten his nickname: the only one the survivors knew him by. Was it on account of his nose, which was eaten away at the end, as if one of his ancestors had had syphillis? Or was it because of some sexual disaster in his military past.

'Sarge,' he broke the heavy silence, 'what we gonna do now?'

'Yeah,' cried another soldier, with his steel-rimmed GI glasses patched with adhesive tape, 'and where in the Sam Hill are we at?'

VD sniffed and looked around the group of GIs shivering in the glade, as if he were trying to imprint their frozen faces on his mind. 'Okay, this is the deal,' he said at last. 'First of all ya gonna quit bitching about being cold and hungry and all the rest of the crap. It's just tough tittie – and nobody can do a goddam thing about it. *Kay?* Second, I don't care a monkey's what ya MOS[1] is. From here on all of you – clerks, cooks, medics, shit-shovellers – you're in the infantry. You're riflemen. *Kay?* Third, what we gonna do?' He stared at them challengingly. 'Well, we're in Indian country now. I don't have to tell you that the Krauts are everywhere down there on the roads. So, we'd better start earning our pay and go hunting Kraut. *Kay?*' He grinned at them contemptuously, as if he knew the fearful thoughts racing through their minds at this moment. 'But don't worry, guys, old VD here'll see you through.' He twisted round and unhitched his canteen. 'Okay, before we take off, let's have a slug of good old kickapoo. It's cold, I know, but I made it myself and I can guarantee it'll take the skin off'n ya teeth.' He lifted the canteen and took a hearty drink of the fiery liquor, made of GI alcohol, ration lemonade powder and a dash of water.

He belched and wiped the back of his dirty hand across his mouth, his faded blue eyes glowing suddenly. 'Here, Ikey,' he thrust the canteen at Rosenbloom, 'wrap yourself round that and pass it on – there's no prejudice in old VD's outfit.'

Rosenbloom hesitated. He thought of the hard little NCO's nickname; then the desire for a drink overcame him. Greedily he raised the canteen to his lips. But he was not fated to drink from it.

'Hit the dirt!' the NCO yelled frantically. 'Get your goddam butts down – *quick*!' With a vicious blow, he knocked the canteen out of Rosenbloom's hands and pushed the startled cook to the snow. 'Can't you goddam well hear,' he gasped, throwing himself beside the other man, '*planes!*'

*   *   *

Half a mile away, Wotan heard them too. They appeared be-

[1] Military specialization. (*Transl.*)

neath the cloud base, as if from nowhere, seeming to hover there, poised to fall on the prey directly beneath them.

Down below, the sleeping grenadiers came to life. In their scores they dropped over the sides of the suddenly halted half-tracks and doubled for the cover of the woods. On the Tigers, the gunners swung up their machine-guns, their icy lethargy gone. Further back, the flak men fumbled frantically with their quadruple cannon, while von Dodenburg groaned inwardly, knowing this his column was trapped.

'Here they come,' Matz yelled, the spandau resting on a protesting Sepp's right shoulder, while his fellow front-runner, as morose as ever, crouched next to him ready to feed in the long gleaming belt of bullets.

The Mustang's leader waggled his wings. Once, twice, three times. It was the signal to start the dive-bombing attack. Screaming in at 400 mph in a shallow dive, the flight leader headed straight for the stalled column. The flak cannons began to chatter frantically. Next to von Dodenburg Matz opened up with a vicious burst. Then just as it seemed that the Ami fighter-bomber must crash into the column, it levelled out with a heightened scream of its protesting motor. For a moment nothing happened. What looked like black eggs began to tumble from its fat belly, turning and revolving wildly and haphazardly as they came closer and closer to the ground. The first load straddled two Tigers at the rear of the column. The turret of the second one – all ten tons of it – was lifted twenty metres into the air and thrown crazily into a nearby field. Next instant, the eighty odd rounds of 88 mm ammunition it carried exploded with a thick crump.

Crouched next to the Volkswagen jeep, von Dodenburg groaned as the Mustangs came in again and again, pressing home their attack with reckless abandon. Twice the flak-gunners managed to hit one of the low-level fighter bombers, but even they returned to the attack. It was only when the squadron leader was hit by a low-level burst and shattered into a million pieces on the far side of the valley, snuffed out like a sudden candle in a gigantic puff of white smoke, that they ended their disastrous bombing.

The shaken tankers and grenadiers had just begun to crawl from their hiding places and start to survey the smoking wreck of the column, when the Mitchells, twin-engined medium bombers, came winging in at less than two hundred metres. All hell broke loose on the Werbomont road, as the 500 lb bombs came tumbling out of their gleaming silver bellies in deadly profusion. The flak hit one and it came swooping in, thick white smoke pouring from its port engine, still dropping its bombs. A small black figure sprang from its side. But the Ami's parachute failed to open. Whirling over and over, hands clasped around his knees like a circus acrobat, the Ami struck the ground at a tremendous speed.

'Hope it gives him a shitty headache!' Schulze yelled above the roar.

But von Dodenburg was oblivious, for the bombers were directly above them now, and the world had turned into a howling, screaming, earth-shaking, nightmare. Frantically he clutched at the jeep's wheel but the explosion of a bomb tore it from his hands. He screamed with agony, as the nails were ripped from his fingers. Acrid yellow smoke filled his lungs. He fought for breath, blinded by the fumes. Another salvo straddled the front of the convoy. A Tiger sagged to one side, greedy flames starting from its shattered engine. A half-track rose a metre into the air and crashed down, splintering every single sprocket wheel, as if they were made of matchwood – and not Krupp steel, while a body flew past them and smashed brokenly against a tree.

Then the earth came up to meet von Dodenburg lying there stretched full length beside the jeep and something slapped him hard in the face. He shook his head. Silver and red stars exploded in front of his closed eyes. He shook his head again. The stars danced even more frantically. The red mist behind them swept forward. He tried to fight it off but it engulfed him, shutting out the noise, the murder and the mayhem all around him.

* * *

'*Oh, my God,*' von Dodenburg groaned weakly, raising himself to his feet, one hand clasped to his aching head, 'what a mess!'

Schulze who had brought him round nodded numbly. 'It's not a mess, sir,' he said through bloodied lips, bruised where the side of the jeep had struck him in the mouth, 'it's a shitty massacre!'

Von Dodenburg knew he was right, even before his eyes had begun to focus correctly. The whole column was burning, scattered along the debris-littered road like a collection of old junk, with the dead sprawled out in the snowy fields on both sides. Here and there an NCO or an officer was attempting to put out the flames or drag a wounded man out of some shattered vehicle. But for the most part, the men in their singed, blackened uniforms, stood there numbly in the snow, staring vacantly at the wrecked column.

'Matz and the front runners?' queried von Dodenburg, not taking his shocked gaze off the convoy.

'They're all right, sir,' Schulze answered. 'They took off into the woods in the end.'

'Good, then get me Major Harsch. We've got to start getting things organized. I want details of casualties, road-worthy vehicles . . . We must get the hell out of here before nightfall. Those fires will advertize our presence for kilometres. And we don't want any more visits from winged Ami friends, do we?'

'You ain't shitting, sir!' Schulze answered grimly. 'I've had enough of those flying bastards!'

While the little American squad under VD watched from high above on the far hillside, the survivors rushed back and forth, dragging out dead and wounded, trying – mostly in vain – to put out the flames, driving what few vehicles had survived to safety further up the road, frantic to be away from the accursed valley road before the fires attracted fresh Ami attacks.

Just before the December evening finally blacked out the valley von Dodenburg was able to take stock of his position, his anxious eyes flashing back and forth from the sky to the long line of walking wounded, leaning wearily against the snowy bank opposite. 'Well, Harsch, how many men have you left?'

Harsch, his once immaculate breeches charred and holed, a bloody bandage round his head, answered woodenly: 'One hundred unwounded, sixty capable of marching though wounded, prepared to fight on for Führer—'

'For God's sake, Harsch,' von Dodenburg held up his hand wearily. 'Spare me heroics. We're not playing soldiers now. What's your vehicle situation?'

Harsch flushed. 'Two – the ones you can see up there.'

'And our tank strength, Schulze?'

'You can count it on the fingers of one hand, sir. Four, plus the Ami Sherman.'

'I see – and crews?'

'We can man 'em all right, sir, if you include a couple of the lightly wounded men—'

'Don't worry, sir,' Matz interrupted. 'I can always drive one of the bastards again now, if you need me to.' He slapped the sturdy fencepole he had strapped to his stump with a soldier's belt. 'This peg-leg is as good as any fancy store-made one.'

Von Dodenburg forced a weary smile and pressed his shoulder. 'Thank you, Matz.' Then he turned to the wounded. What was he going to do with them? With the vehicles at his disposal, he could just about transport the survivors, if he spread the surplus grenadiers over the tanks. But there would be no room for the wounded.

Slowly he crunched across the snow, now beginning to harden in the tight valley as it grew darker. For a long moment he stared at their ashen, exhausted faces. Was it only a month since they had marched into camp, singing so confidently, their step firm, bodies bursting with strength and good health? Now they looked ten years older, the lustre gone out of their eyes, their bodies shrunken and frail.

'Comrades,' he said softly. 'I think I don't have to tell you our position? We have suffered a grievous blow. Many of your comrades have made the supreme sacrifice for the Homeland. Our transport has been shattered. You have spilled your blood in an uneven battle . . .' He hesitated and licked his dry lips. 'But that battle must go on. Our objective *must* be achieved. Do you know what that means?'

A bareheaded grenadier, with a blood-soaked bandage over the empty socket where his right eye had once been, answered at once, a trace of that old fanatical Hitler Youth enthusiasm in his young voice. 'It means, sir, that we are useless to you – a drag on the rest of you.'

Von Dodenburg nodded. 'Correct, comrade. We only have sufficient transport for those who can fight.'

'What do you want us to do, sir? Make our own way back to our own lines.'

Von Dodenburg swallowed and told himself again just what a hypocrite he was to abuse their youthful enthusiasm thus. 'Yes, something like that. The Amis to our rear are thoroughly disorganized. It would be a matter of working your way through their patrols and contacting our forward elements.'

'And where might they be, roughly sir?' asked a blond giant, with his arm in a sling.

'I can't say exactly,' von Dodenburg lied. 'But my guess is that they'll be in Stavelot now, perhaps even in Trois Ponts, with a bit of luck.'

The blond giant forced a tired smile then winced in pain. 'Well, that's not so bad sir. A matter of ten or fifteen kilometres, that's all. Why, we used to do that before breakfast in the Hitler Youth.'

'Yes, that would be about the distance,' von Dodenburg agreed slowly, as if he were giving serious consideration to the problem, knowing all the time that at night, wounded, confronted with temperatures way below zero as well as Ami patrols, there wouldn't be many of the men facing him so cheerfully at this moment who would make those fifteen kilometres – if it were only fifteen kilometres. Hastily he repressed his disgust with himself, trying to be confident and businesslike. 'Naturally you just can't wander out of here and hope for the best. My suggestion is that you split into groups, evenly divided between less and more serious wounds, each led by an NCO. Perhaps not more than ten men in one group at the most—'

'I'll take a group,' Sergeant Ochmann interrupted him, raising his shattered hand. 'I'm used to these conditions, sir. I was with you in Popovland, if you recall?'

Colonel von Dodenburg did indeed recall Sergeant Ochmann's service in Russia; he had been accused of raping a twelve-year-old peasant girl and had just escaped being sentenced to Torgau because a Russian partisan had shot his eye out the very next day. 'All right then, you can take them, Ochmann. But remember, keep off the main roads – and don't let them bunch. That would be asking for trouble.'

'You can rely on me,' replied the one-eyed sergeant. 'I'll get them through, if it's the last thing I do.'

Schulze broke wind loudly and insolently. Ochmann flushed and opened his mouth to say something, but von Dodenburg beat him to it. There was no more time to be wasted. 'Goodbye, lads, you'd better be off.' He touched his hand to his peaked cap as if in salute. 'I'll see you all again in the Homeland.'

They shuffled to a pathetic semblance of attention. 'We'll be marching with you on the victory parade down the *Unter den Linden*, sir,' said the blond giant.

Von Dodenburg grinned. 'Of course – the victory parade.'

They turned. Slowly they started the long trail back the way they had come. High above them on the snowy hillside, the little group of men crouched around the bandy sergeant watched their progress down the road.

'There they go,' VD commented hoarsely, 'the halt, the lame and the blind.' He clapped his calloused hand against the butt of the carbine, and looked significantly at Rosenbloom. 'I guess, Ikey, we're gonna have a real old Texas-style turkey shoot this night, eh.' He chuckled softly.

Far below, von Dodenburg watched the wounded's slow weary progress until he could see them no longer. Then slowly he turned to the waiting survivors. There weren't many of them left for the task in front of them, but he had to capture that vital bridge, even if he were down to his last man and his last tank.

'All right, men, mount up!'

'Come on you asparagus Tarzans, move those fat arses of yours! *Mount up!*' Schulze added in an urgent bellow.

The motors burst throatily into life. The grenadiers clambered over the sides of the half-tracks or perched themselves on the Tigers' decks, heads buried in their camouflaged jackets, ready for the freezing night journey ahead of them. Matz, followed by Sepp chewing on a piece of charred meat and Hairless Harry, stumped on his new found peg-leg towards the Sherman. Von Dodenburg took one last look behind him, past the ruined convoy. There was nothing to be seen.

As the long black fingers of the night started to slide into the winter white of the silent valley and cover the young dead, the first faint crackle and snap of small arms fire indicated what was happening to the walking wounded and the little convoy began to roll westwards again in the lethal race for Huy Bridge.

4

Tuesday, December 19th 1944.

The white-helmeted MPs guarding the door of Hodges' new HQ at Chaudfontaine gawped. The man who was emerging from the old-fashioned British staff car was dressed in the strangest Allied uniform they had ever seen: suede boots, baggy corduroy civilian slacks, a camouflaged para jacket with a flowered scarf taking the place of a necktie, and a sloppy red British para beret pulled down low over his forehead. And in one hand he held a rusty black umbrella.

Then the MP sergeant recognized him. 'Jesus,' he breathed, '*it's Monty!*'

With a casual salute – almost a wave – the British Field Marshal, followed by an aide carrying a wicker-work basket, swept by the rigid MPs. 'Awful weather, isn't it?' he remarked. 'Pity you chaps have to be out in it.'

A moment later Montgomery was looking round the grave-faced officers of Hodges' staff, grouped behind their silver-haired commander, 'Well, gentlemen. I gather a difficult situation has arisen.' He nodded to the aide. The young officer quickly pushed a chair towards him. The Field Marshal sat down and held out his hand for the wicker-work basket. Opening it, he took out a salad sandwich. 'Now then,' he said brightly, 'do tell me the form.'

While Hodges explained the situation on the northern flank of what was now being called the Battle of the Bulge, the little Englishman with the beaked nose listened attentively, chewing solidly on his lettuce sandwiches, pausing now and again to nod his head.

Hodges looked at Montgomery and waited. The Britisher handed back the wicker basket to the attentive aide. He cleared his throat. 'Very interesting, General, very interesting,' he said. 'But naturally quite impossibly untidy.'

Hodges' tired eyes lit up angrily for a moment. 'What do you mean, Field Marshal?'

'My dear General Hodges, we simply don't have the reserves to cover the whole front. We must make a decision as to the German objective on the Meuse and group there.'

'But that would mean—'

The little Field Marshal beat him to it. 'That would mean a withdrawal on some other sector of the front.'

'No,' said Hodges firmly, taking the suggestion almost as if it were a personal insult. 'American troops never withdraw.'

'What, in your opinion, Hodges, is the direction of the main German panzer thrust?'

Hodges pulled himself together. He needed help, he knew that, and the victor of El Alamein was the only man in the Allied camp who could give it him, especially as he had the whole resources of the British Second Army at his disposal, which could be thrown in to defend the Meuse if the worst came to the worst. 'Our guess, Field Marshal, is that the German point is heading for Liège.' He thrust his forefinger at the industrial town lying on the Meuse. 'Late yesterday evening, Ninth TAC stopped a German armoured column heading that way – or most of it, that is.'

Montgomery shook his head. 'Out of the question – quite out of the question, Hodges. *Our* intelligence has picked up the information that the Luftwaffe has orders *not* to bomb the bridges *south* of Liège. And I believe the flying bombs are still hitting that city. You can see what that adds up to, can't you? Liège doesn't enter their calculations.' Leaning over, he poked his own finger at the big map. 'This is the Boche objective – here at Huy.' Without waiting for any further objection, he rattled on. 'Now this is what we'll do. We'll clear out your chaps swanning around in the Ambleve valley. They can be used to shore up the shoulders of the bulge, what? I've already ordered Horrocks[1] to bring his fellows down from Holland and back you up on the west bank of the Meuse. Then we must mass our reserves in the north-west to give the Jerry what for when the time is

[1] General Horrocks, commander of the British Thirty Corps. (*Transl.*)

ripe. But he hasn't shot his bolt yet by a long chalk.' He rose and pursed his thin lips thoughtfully for a moment, while Hodges and his officers waited impatiently for him to speak. 'And by the way, you'd better see off that Boche chappie in the Ambleve Valley or he'll jolly well have your bridge, won't he?'

* * *

The killings had started without warning. They had hardly left the rest, limping painfully through the snow, on their way back to their own lines when the first vicious volley had crashed into their surprised ranks. Thereafter it had gone on all night. The wounded, their number getting pitifully smaller, had tried to throw off their pursuers by every trick they knew. But wounded as they were, they were no match for their unseen assailants. Again and again, they thought they had thrown them off, only to be met by a fresh burst of machine-gun fire, as they emerged from their new cover.

Now Ochmann, gasping with effort, his wound bleeding once more, was at the end of his tether. He had long abandoned what was left of his slower moving charges. He knew that with them he didn't stand a chance in hell; and one thing Sergeant Ochmann was sure of – come what may, he intended to save his own skin. But now as he blundered blindly through the grey gloom of the fir forest, ploughing through the waist-deep snow, his helmet and rifle gone, the pistol on his belt his only weapon, he knew that he couldn't keep going much longer.

But what was he to do?

As the sound of his pursuers grew louder, their feet crashing through the snowy undergrowth, his mind raced frantically, trying to solve that problem. In Russia he had blessed that unknown partisan who had blown out his eye: unwittingly the man had saved him from a court-martial, and even worse, perhaps another winter in that Russian hell. But what could save him now?

Then, with the instant clarity of a vision, he had it. Sergeant Hans Ochmann ceased running. His chest heaving wildly, yet with a faint knowing smile on his cunning face, he turned to meet his pursuers, his hands above his head.

A moment later, a red-faced Rosenbloom burst from the undergrowth, Tommy gun clenched in his hands. Instinctively he raised it and pressed the trigger. Nothing happened. 'Christ on a crutch,' he cursed violently. 'A crappy stoppage!'

Ochmann breathed out a wild sigh of relief. He had been saved from death in the nick of time. It seemed like a sign from the heaven in which he had not believed since his childhood.

'Don't shoot,' he yelled wildly in English 'Don't shoot! I have been to America. I have a brother in Milwaukee.'

'Yeah, and I've got a pregnant sister in New Jersey,' VD said cynically, joining Rosenbloom in the glade. 'Come on, Ikey, what the hell are you waiting for man – a crappy written invitation?'

Angrily Rosenbloom fumbled with the sub-machine gun, jerking back the bolt, trying to clear the obstruction. During the night-long 'Texas-style Turkey Shoot', he must have slaughtered at least eight of the German wounded with it; he couldn't understand why it was letting him down now.

Ochmann swallowed frantically. He dropped to his knees in the snow, tears streaming down his cheek from his good eye, wringing his hands in the classic gesture of supplication. 'Please . . . please, don't shoot me – *please*!'

VD looked down at him contemptuously. 'You should have thought of that when you shot our guys down in cold blood,' he snarled. 'Christ, I thought you was an SS trooper. Try to behave like one.'

'But I can help you,' Ochmann stammered as Rosenbloom started to bring the tommy-gun to bear upon him again. 'Believe me, I know something very important for your commanders.'

VD knocked Rosenbloom's weapon away. An angry burst hissed harmlessly into the snow-heavy firs. Ochmann screamed with fear.

'What did you say, Kraut?' VD stepped forward and grabbed Ochmann's hair. He forced his one-eyed, tear-stained face upwards. 'You'd better not be shitting me, Kraut,' he murmured through gritted yellow teeth. 'Now piss or get off the pot!'

'They're heading for the bridge at Huy,' Ochmann whined 'Their orders are to seize it . . . When they've done that, the rest of our Sixth SS Panzer Army will follow up,' He gasped with relief and broke off as the tough little American NCO let go of his hair. He let his head fall and sobbed.

VD looked at Rosenbloom and the rest of the platoon who had now joined them in the snowy glade. 'Do you hear that?' he said slowly, biting the edge of his bottom lip. 'Them SS bastards are heading for the Meuse bridge.'

'But what can we do?' asked the bespectacled ex-medic. 'Hell, we ain't got nothing but our side-arms and these.' He indicated their rifles and grease-guns. 'The Krauts have still got tanks.'

'Sure,' VD said calmly. 'I've heard that one before – all my goddam life. What can we do, cos we've only got—' He broke off scornfully. 'Yeah, when you think like that, soldier, you might as well give up right from the goddam start. Of course, we can do something. We can trail those Heinies until we hit our own guys. Then we can tell them what the bastards are gonna do.'

'But the Krauts took off hours ago – and they got wheels,' Rosenbloom objected. 'The trail'll be as dead as this bastard here will be in one minute flat.'

The little noncom shook his head slowly. 'Do you guys know why they call me VD in the Regular Army?' He paused, while Ochmann continued to sob on his knees next to him. 'You Joes think it was because I got the pox, eh? Well, I'm not denying I ain't had a dose of clap now and again. It's an occupational hazard in the Regular Army, cos decent girls' – he said the words as if they were in italics – 'don't want guys like me. Rough soldiers. Ner, so all we're left with is the cathouses and B-girls.' He spat thickly into the scuffed snow, narrowly missing Rosenbloom's boots. 'No, I'll tell yer where I got that nickname. In the Islands in forty-one just after Pearl. When the Nips came, me and a bunch of other guys started to hike from one end of the place to the other. We thought we'd get away with a boat or something. *I* did,' he poked a dirty thumb at his chest. 'The rest didn't – they gave in. That's why I'm alive today, and them poor bastards is dead or in some cruddy Nip prison cage. So you know what they did in records when I got to Australia, they stamped them "VD".'

'But what the hell does it mean, Sarge?' the medic broke in.

'VD? Why – very-goddam-determined! That's what it means.' He aimed a vicious kick at Ochmann's ribs. 'Get up, you Kraut bastard. I've got a job for you.'

Still sobbing, but aware now that somehow or other, his life had been spared by the tough little Ami NCO, Ochmann stumbled blindly to his feet.

'You see,' VD continued, 'we've got a guide here. He knows the route the rest are gonna take – and we're gonna follow that route. And when the time is ripe, we'll hand that fancy-panted Kraut Colonel of theirs over on a nice big silver platter.' He slung his carbine over his shoulder and shoved Ochmann in front of him. 'Okay, Kraut, move it. You've gone and gotten yourself a job with good old Uncle Sugar – and if you're good, you might even live long enough to draw your pay. *March*.'

* * *

At dawn they had circled Werbomont, guided by the two front-runners, who seemed to know every single forest trail and back road, for which a worried von Dodenburg was very grateful; then he knew he could no longer afford to risk head-on confrontations with the enemy. Though as it grew increasingly light on that grey December morning, the countryside, dotted here and there by abandoned farms and hamlets seemed strangely empty of enemy soldiers, as if the Amis had completely withdrawn. It was almost as if the snow-bound, stark Belgian countryside in front of them had been left to its fate by both civilians and soldiers, given voluntarily to the handful of weary men who now ploughed the deep snow of its back roads and forest trails.

At ten von Dodenburg decided it was time to call a halt. Hidden by a line of great oaks, which in summer undoubtedly afforded pleasant shade on the little Belgian road, he allowed the men to get down from the vehicles to stretch their legs, grab a brief meal, while he attempted to raise Army HQ. But the harassed operator tried in vain to reach the Sixth SS's Command Post, while a haggard unshaven von Dodenburg chain-smoked looted *Camels* until his empty stomach started to retch drily at the powerful smoke.

And then the young operator started visibly. 'Sir,' he yelled from within the half-track.

Von Dodenburg threw away his half-smoked cigarette. 'Have you got them?'

'Yessir. And more,' the radio operator said proudly. 'I've got the Army Commander – General Dietrich!'

'Give me here.' Von Dodenburg picked up the earphones and slipped them over his head swiftly. 'Von Dodenburg here,' he snapped, forgetting all radio procedure. 'Sir.'

'Damned good to hear you, Dodenburg,' Dietrich's thick Bavarian voice came through, faint but audible. 'We've got a fix on your position. You've done splendidly in spite of everything.'

'Thank you, sir. Twenty more kilometres and we're there.'

'Yes. That is about my estimate.'

Kraemer's you mean, von Dodenburg thought, but he didn't tell the Army Commander that. Instead he said. 'But we're in a piss-poor situation, sir. I've suffered serious casualties and I'm very short on transport. I really don't know if I've got the muscle to tackle the objective.'

'You can't let me down now, Dodenburg,' the Butcher Boy said urgently. 'Everything depends upon your capturing that—' he caught himself in time in case the American monitors were listening. 'All morning the Führer HQ has been on my back pestering me with "when are you going to get it".'

'I can appreciate that, sir,' von Dodenburg answered, a little angry at the Army Commander's inability to understand his position; it was typical of the base stallions at HQ. 'But I need muscle – *muscle*!'

'And you'll get it, Dodenburg, I promise you. Positions five and six are back in our hands—' his listener knew that meant Stavelot and Trois Ponts – 'and we're on the move again. I've diverted a regiment of the Reich to help you. The Amis are falling back everywhere. All I need is that damned objective.

Get me it and it will be the Diamonds[1] for you and the Cross in Gold for everyone of your men. I'll see you're knee-deep in whores and booze for a solid month after this offensive is over.'

Von Dodenburg laughed. 'Thank you, sir, but looking at my men at the moment, I hardly think most of them would be capable of getting it up. A bowl of pea soup and a cup of hot nigger sweat would be more in their line.'

'I can appreciate that, Dodenburg. But get me that objective. Not only for me, but for the German people—'

The radio went dead. Angrily von Dodenburg summoned the operator, but although he did his sweating, frantic best, he could not get the set to work again. In the end he threw down his screwdriver with a curse of rage, 'Like everything else in these conditions, sir – it's just shitting well fallen to bits.'

Von Dodenburg forced a smile and clapped the angry, red-faced young man on the shoulder. 'Thank you all the same. You did your best. See if you can get yourself a cup of nigger sweat.'

The radio operator went away, grateful for the opportunity afforded him to get out of the freezing half-track, leaving von Dodenburg alone with his thoughts. What was he to do? Should he press on with so few men under his command? Wasn't that inviting disaster? Wouldn't it result only in the sacrificing of their young lives for no return? He stared out of the half-track. Starving Sepp was stirring a fresh mixture of soil and gas in an old tin to the consistency of a thin porridge before lighting it beneath his last can of Old Man. Next to him Matz and Schulze were engaged in one of their interminable but good-humoured quarrels. Around them the grenadiers squatted or crouched in the snow, smoking slowly or chatting to one another in tired subdued voices, dark rings of exhaustion under their eyes. How young they looked, he told himself, mere boys.

Yet could he put their lives before those of the many millions of old men, women and children back in the Homeland, who although they did not even know of the existence of this hand-

[1] The highest category of the Knight's Cross. (*Transl.*)

ful of boys or their desperate situation, relied upon them totally? For if this last offensive failed, Germany would go under – there was no denying that hard truth – and those same people would be subjected to an alien tyranny. He could remember the great days nearly five years before when a similar handful of weary young men under his command[1] had conquered a tremendous fortress against overwhelming odds and opened the door westwards for the German Army to conquer France. A lot of water had flown under the bridge since then. He had grown personally tired and a little cynical – there had been too many campaigns, too many defeats, too much blood-letting – yet couldn't he do it one more time – just one more time?

As the first flakes of the new snow started to drift down sadly, he was overcome by burning hope. Dropping out of the half-track, he cupped his hands over his mouth and yelled: 'All right, lads, let's roll them! This snow is just the sort of cover we need to get to the bridge! *Mount up everywhere!*'

* * *

They passed through the vast empty landscape like a trail of insignificant black ants. The country breathed hostility. Conditions were terrible on the back roads which the two front-runners found for the Wotan. The observation panels froze over in the howling, snow-filled wind, blinding the helpless drivers. Time and again, they lost control of their vehicles so that they danced crazily across the road, slewing round and round, missing the ditches by a hair's breadth, snapping off the snow-laden firs like matchwood with their long cannon.

Once a half-track landed in a ditch. With fingers that felt like enormously swollen sausages, the shivering grenadiers attached a steel hawser to it from the Sherman, whose rubber tracks provided better traction on the snow. But when the Ami tank took the strain, the hawser parted like a piece of wet cotton; and they were forced to push the half-track out by main force.

Panting and broken-lunged they stumbled back into their

[1] See Leo Kessler: *SS Panzer Battalion* for further details. (*Transl.*)

vehicles and crawled on. The wind was by now laying an icy layer over cannon, decks, bodies. Men wept with the pain of the cold. Icicles hung from their beards. Nostrils froze. Every fresh breath was like a knife-stab to the lungs. To touch the metal of the vehicles was to touch a red-hot poker, which ripped the flesh off their fingers. Here and there, a young soldier, the tears frozen to his ashen cheeks like cold pearls, closed his eyes and prayed for death to release him.

And then when it seemed that the cruel torture could only end in death, the snow storm ceased. Only a matter of seconds later – or so it seemed to the exhausted, pathetic young soldiers now daring to open their eyes and break the ice-crust which had formed over them – a thin, watery sun slid into a suddenly hard blue winter sky. But it wasn't the sun that caught their attention. It was the cluster of houses, grouped round the onion-towered church about a kilometre away, and beyond them, the long dull-gleaming snake of the river.

'Holy shit,' Schulze breathed, the suddenly melting ice sliding down his broad face, 'we've done it, sir.'

Von Dodenburg nodded slowly. In a voice which was little better than an old man's croak, he said. 'Yes, the Meuse . . . at last.'

*   *   *

Thirty minutes later they had scouted the village and ascertained that it had been abandoned. With Sepp and Hairless Harry as guides, they explored the poor little peasant houses. But they were not suitable for their needs. As Sepp, now chewing happily on a wrinkled ancient apple he had looted from some peasant's store, remarked: 'They're too poor around here to even have a pot to piss in.'

Von Dodenburg nodded. 'You're right.' He thought for a moment, staring at the Baroque church, its slate-covered onion tower gleaming now in the thin cold rays of the wintery sun. 'All right, we'll use the church. But the tanks and half-tracks go in first. We don't want the Ami planes to spot us again – after yesterday. Then the men can follow.'

Hairless Harry, the strict Catholic from the pious canton of

St Vith, stared at the Colonel aghast. 'But, sir,' he protested, 'you can't use the holy church as a billet ... That's sacrilege!'

'Go on,' Sepp sneered, tossing away his core, 'holy Joe – what do you think the priests do in there?' He made an obscene rubbing movement with his right hand. 'That's what.'

For once Hairless Harry ignored him. As the first tank crashed into the great eighteenth century wooden door, he muttered grimly. 'No good'll come of this, no good at all...'

But a few minutes later, the happy grenadiers, overjoyed to get out of the snow, had no eyes for their strange surroundings or ears for Hairless Harry's dour warning. The nave was full of warmth, noise, smoke and laughter. On the floor a fire had been lit and a group of noisy grenadiers was busy keeping it supplied with fuel, by chopping up the dark, polished pews with their axes. Others were opening up the last cans of Old Man, tossing the empty tins causally over their shoulders into the pulpit. At the altar, Schulze, in his stocking feet, both big toes peering out of the holed synthetic material, was hanging up his boots to dry over the little fire he had lit. Near him a happy Sepp was swallowing communion tablet after tablet, washing the dry fodder down with sips of the priest's communion wine from a gilted goblet. Further on, a group of grenadiers, who had discovered a bottle of the colourless powerful local cherry-stone schnapps, were singing that song about 'Auntie Hedwig', who had tried to work her 'sewing machine all night' and had failed, using up 'all her oil'; while Hairless Harry, standing alone in the middle of the white-painted nave stared at them in open-mouthed horror.

Von Dodenburg finished warming his hands and nodded to the waiting Harsch whose binoculars were already hanging around his neck. 'You ready, Harsch?'

'Yessir,'

'Good.' Von Dodenburg picked up Schulze's machine-pistol and indicated to the big NCO, who liked to act as his bodyguard, that he was going. Schulze pulled a face, but as he was barefoot there was little he could do. Together the two officers passed outside and worked their way carefully through the village, their eyes constantly flashing up to the deep-blue sky to check for the dreaded Ami fighter-bombers. But the winter sky was empty and thirty minutes later they reached the spot where they had planned to carry out their preliminary recce, without being spotted.

Hidden behind a snow-covered, broken-wheeled farm cart, shading any tell-tale gleam of their binoculars with one hand, they surveyed the river. The bridge – an old-fashioned double span iron structure – was guarded. That was clear. Dark uniformed figures moved back and forth across it, and on the west bank he could make out sand-bagged mg nests at the bridge's entrance. He swung his glasses round carefully. Between the tall, red-brick houses lining the far bank, he could make out dark bulky shapes, poorly camouflaged under snow-heavy nets. Men were moving around them with shovels, clearing away the snow. 'Churchills,' he whispered to Harsch, as if the men on the other bank might hear. 'Must be British.'

'The Amis must be running out of manpower. It's a good sign.'

Von Dodenburg grunted and adjusted his glasses, lining them on the nearside bank. Slowly and systematically he started to sweep the riverside. What he saw didn't particularly please him.

'That approach is our weak support, Major. Once we're on the bridge itself, I am confident our men will capture it – and even if they blow the damned thing in our faces, our follow-up engineers will be able to construct a new one. No,' he bit his bottom lip. 'It's that damned approach road that worries me.'

'How do you mean, sir?' Harsch asked, not lowering his glasses.

'You see how it makes that ninety degree angle before it runs on to the bridge itself . . . where those two great rocks flank the road . . . Get it, Harsch?'

Harsch, focused his glasses on the hair-pin bend dominated by two sheer slabs of rock worn black and smooth by the passage of time, their tops crowned in a heavy cap of snow. 'I can see it, sir.'

'Well, that's where they could well grab us by the short and curlies as the soldiers say. A determined group of men with a couple of mgs and an anti-tank gun posted there could hold us up all day. You see there is no room for our tanks to manoeuvre. They'd have to approach one by one and take their medicine as it is spooned out to them. And it wouldn't be very nice medicine, I can tell you, Harsch.'

Harsch lowered his glasses and looked at him. 'Send in my panzer grenadiers first, sir,' he suggested, tight-lipped. 'If there were any Ami attempt to block the tanks' approach, they'd clear it away quickly enough.'

'That is what I have been thinking, Harsch. But the action – if it came to that – would have to be sharp and effective. We couldn't afford to allow the Tommies to bring up any reserves. They might not be very aggressive soldiers, but they are devils in defence.'

Harsch's face set in a sneer. 'I don't think you have anything to worry about on that score. The Tommies are no match for my men, sir. My grenadiers won't let you down.'

'I hope you're right,' von Dodenburg said. 'Now come on, let's get out of here – my feet are like ice.'

* * *

But Harsch's grenadiers had already let him down in another way, as he learned on returning to the warmth of the church. Schulze, washing his big dirty feet in some hot water he had poured into a baptismal font, and trying in vain to achieve a lather with the iron-hard issue synthetic soap, waited till Harsch had gone, then said urgently. 'Can I speak to you for a moment, sir?'

'Won't it wait? My damned feet are going to fall off at any moment – I could do with a cup of nigger sweat.'

'No, sir,' Schulze said, tugging a great yellow foot out of the font, and wiping it hastily on Matz's undershirt. 'Sparks has just picked up an Ami broadcast from *Soldatensender Calais*[1].'

'Sheer lying propaganda,' von Dodenburg said, wondering all the same what was coming.

[1] A propaganda radio station run by the British journalist Sefton Delmer. (*Transl.*)

'I know, sir,' Schulze said hurriedly. 'But this time they said something that could be easily checked, if it were true or not.'

'What?'

Schulze drew a deep breath. 'That an SS regiment in the Ardennes had murdered its prisoners, a couple of days back. And you know who they said commanded that regiment?'

Even before Schulze finished, von Dodenburg knew – with a sinking feeling – what the name would be.

'Colonel Kuno von Dodenburg!' Schulze said with a sudden rush. '*You sir*, with Wotan as the shitty killers!' . . .

* * *

'Harsch,' von Dodenburg controlled himself with difficulty, 'I have just heard a statement about a broadcast made by the Ami propaganda station *Soldatensender Calais*.'

'I see.'

Von Dodenburg leaned forwards so that the panzer grenadiers slumped wearily against the wall or chatting softly with one another could not hear. 'That statement said Wotan had been concerned with a massacre of Ami POWs a couple of days ago.' He forced his voice to remain calm and emotionless. 'Do you know anything about it, Major?'

Harsch's cold grey eyes lit up momentarily; then the sudden light died away as if an electric current had been switched off. 'Of course, sir,' he said coldly. 'They were only a trashy lot of Jews and cowboys. I didn't want to dirty my hands with them any further. Besides, I simply did not have the transport for them.'

'I see,' breathed von Dodenburg, fighting back his temper. 'How very efficient of you, Major Harsch! Thank you, that's all I wanted to know. Good night.'

He turned and then stopped. 'By the way, Major, let's hope that we capture that bridge tomorrow. For if we don't and we lose this damned war, you and I undoubtedly will hang by the neck from the first Allied gallows. For you have signed both our death warrants by your actions. Good night once again.'

5

Wednesday, December 20th 1944.

A shadow darted from behind one of the little stone peasant cottages. 'All clear, Major,' the scout whispered. 'There are no sentries till right up to the bridge.' The whites of his eyes gleamed against the soot-black of his young face. 'They all seem to be having a bit of shut-eye down there.'

Major Harsch turned to von Dodenburg waiting next to him in the shelter of the little cottage. 'Any further orders, Colonel?'

'No Harsch. All I'm asking of you and your men is to clear the approaches to the bridge without any noise so that I can get a run across before the Tommies get those Churchills of theirs into action. Catch them with their knickers down, Harsch, and the bridge is ours.' He hesitated a fraction. 'Well then, Major, good luck.' He could not bring himself to shake the other man's hand.

'Thank you, sir.'

Harsch took a last look at the vehicles hidden on both sides of the steep cobbled road that led to the Huy bridge, waiting to follow up his grenadiers, then commanded softly: 'All right, men, move out – after me.'

Standing next to Matz, Schulze shook his head and whispered contemptuously, 'Did you hear that, you cripple? Like a fart in a trance he is, that major!'

The young grenadiers, their side-arms muffled in the sacking they had found in the abandoned cottages, moved from the cover of the houses. The icy blast of the wind, knifing across the pre-dawn countryside, struck them immediately. In their thin uniforms they shivered violently and gripped their weapons more firmly, as they stole down the sides of the silent street like grey timber wolves from the winter forest.

Somewhere down below a dog barked at the night sky, high,

harsh and hysterical. Hairless Harry, their guide, started with fear. But there was no angry shout of alarm or sudden burst of tracer. Hairless Harry breathed out with relief.

'It's all right, sir,' he whispered.

Harsch nodded, his machine-pistol held at the ready. He could just make out the outline of the ancient church and great grey bulk of the medieval citadel to the left of the bridge. 'Come on,' he snapped, 'we've no time to waste.'

They passed a burnt-out cottage, from which a tangle of rusty barbed wire ran across the road. The primitive road block held them up only for a matter of seconds. Then they were all through and moving purposefully towards their objective down below. There was no sound from the town across the river. The bridge began to loom larger through the icy gloom.

Major Harsch tightened his grip on the butt of his Schmeisser. He felt no fear, for his mind was far away from the icy cobbled road that led to the bridge, it was in Berlin at the Reich Chancellery, where the Führer himself congratulated him on his successful capture of the vital bridge before handing him the coveted Knight's Cross of the Iron Cross. He could see it now as the Führer took his hand in both of his and looked up at him in admiration, then pronounced those wonderful words: 'My dear Harsch, herewith I appoint you to the—'

At that moment, VD sloshed the jerrican of gas across the pile of wood they had found in the abandoned houses on the heights above the church where the Germans had set up their HQ. 'For Christ's sake, quick Ikey!' he cried urgently.

With trembling hands the ex-cook struck his match and tossed it on to the pile of wood. Bright flame shot into the grey gloom until the entire top of the hillside overlooking the sleeping town seemed to be burning.

'*Who the sodding hell goes there?*' yelled a thick surprised voice from one of the houses before the bridge, but there was no need for an answer. The beacon on the hillside above told the unknown Tommy sentry all. A sudden vicious burst of red tore the stillness apart.

'At the double!' Major Harsch yelled desperately. '*Follow me!*'

The bridge was only a hundred metres away now. Harsch was possessed by the crazed fancy that once he had crossed it, all would be well; the bridge was his path to safety. He must get over it.

A wildly contorted, terrified face under a flat soup-bowl helmet loomed up. He felled the Tommy with a frantic burst from the hip. Another Tommy appeared from nowhere, a rifle clenched in his tense, white fists. Harsch swung the butt of his Schmeisser up and smashed it into the enemy's jaw. There were little groups of cursing, screaming, stabbing, shooting soldiers everywhere, swaying back and forth as they fought to the death, skidding from side to side in the blood on the cobbles like ice-skaters in some terrible fantasy rink. Frightened cries of rage and pain rose everywhere in German and English, while across the river the first throaty coughs of engines attempting to start on an icy December morning indicated that the Tommies were preparing their Churchills for action.

Harsch stopped. 'You,' he gasped to Hairless Harry at his side. 'Give me your grenade – quick, man.'

Harry fumbled with the potato masher and handed it across, shoulders tensed fearfully as if a bullet might strike him at any moment.

'When I throw,' Harsch commanded, trying to control his breathing and tug out the firing ring at the same time, 'follow me in!'

'Sir.'

'*Now*,' Harsch yelled and lobbed the grenade at the twin Vickers holding up the advance 'FOLLOW ME!'

As it exploded in a vicious spurt of scarlet, Harsch doubled forward, firing from thc hip. A Tommy staggered up from the wreckage of the gun-pit. Harsch fired a quick burst. The Tommy's hands fanned the air frantically, as he fell back among his dead comrades, gurgling sickeningly from a windpipe. Another man ran for the SS officer with a long old-fashioned bayonet in his hand. He jammed his butt in the man's face. Something snapped. The Tommy fell without a sound.

'Come on, come on,' Harsch gasped. 'We're nearly there!'

The handful of survivors clattered after him, each man alone in the noise and smoke of battle, gambling blindly with an unknown death. The roar of the Churchills was getting louder by the second. The far side of the bridge was only a matter of metres. Harsch was already mentally allotting his handful of men to their defence positions. Twenty metres more and he would have done it.

A group of Tommies ahead of them were trying to set up a Bren machine-gun. Behind them a bare-headed man ran out of a house, a strange-looking bell-barrelled pistol in his hand. The clank of the Churchills was frighteningly close. The man with the strange pistol stood there, strangely undecided, legs spread apart, as if he wanted to stop the rush across the bridge with his body alone. The first ugly metal bulk of a Churchill swung round the corner at a right angle. Still the man with the pistol, the lone survivor of the defending force, did not react.

'Damned fool!' Harsch yelled and pressed the Schmeisser's trigger. The white tracer cut the air hysterically. And missed. The Tommy flinched. But he did not move out of their path. Now Harsch knew they would make the other side of the bridge before the Churchill. 'Smoke,' he yelled and stopped, his lungs threatening to burst. 'Throw a smoke grenade!'

A young grenadier behind tugged a phosphorous grenade from his belt and threw it in a high arc towards the tank. It exploded with a white puff of smoke in front of the Churchill. Thick clouds of smoke started to pour from it blinding the tank driver, and still the bareheaded Tommy did not move. Slowly, triumphantly, Major Harsch raised his machine-pistol to finish him off. Almost pleasurably, trying to control the trip-hammer action of his wildly beating heart, he crooked his finger round the trigger and squeezed. Nothing happened. He wrenched at the trigger again. Nothing! Ten metres away the silent Tommy started to raise his pistol and Harsch recognized the weapon for what it was.

'Kill him – in three devil's name KILL—'

His desperate cry died on his lips as the man fired, and a blinding light exploded before his eyes. He screamed as the flame ate his face. Yelling, he clawed at the suddenly empty sockets, trying to extinguish the pain of the charred flesh. But there was no way to put it out.

* * *

'Sir . . . sir!' called Hairless Harry, the blood streaming down the side of his shining naked skull. 'They failed . . . It's all over . . .'

Schulze grabbed him in his big arms, as he attempted to run past the CO. 'All right, all right, knock it off!' he yelled. He freed one of his big hands and holding the terrified Belgian renegade, as if he were a baby, slapped his ashen face. 'Now, come on, snap out of it, you stupid shit!'

Schulze swung him round to face a waiting von Dodenburg. Behind them the five tanks were ticking over softly, as their drivers waited for the order to advance. 'I'll feed you a knuckle sandwich, if you don't tell the CO what happened down there, mate,' he said threateningly, doubling up his massive fist.

The face of the Belgian renegade blanched with fear.

'Well?' Schulze demanded, while von Dodenburg waited silently.

'It was terrible, sir,' stammered Hairless Harry. 'We didn't have a chance once we were on the bridge . . . fought to the last. But they were too much for us,' his words tailed away.

'Fought to the last,' Schulze spat scornfully. 'So what are you doing here, mate,' he demanded. 'I can't see no fucking wings sprouting from your shoulders!'

'Be quiet,' von Dodenburg snapped. From below he could just make out the faint noise of the Tommy tanks. 'What happened to Major Harsch?'

'Dead – they're all dead.'

Von Dodenburg nodded to Sepp. The other Belgian stuffed the last of his sausage into his greedy mouth and led his compatriot to one side.

For a moment there was no sound save the wind and the cawing of the rooks in the stark-black naked oaks. Soon it would be dawn and von Dodenburg knew he must act fast if he were to capture the bridge before the Tommies brought up reinforcements.

'Are we going to have another go, sir?' Schulze broke into his thoughts. 'It ain't much, this lot.' He extended his big hand at the five tanks and couple of half-tracks.

Von Dodenburg nodded grimly. 'I know, Schulze. You don't have to draw me a picture. But we must.' He bit his lip. 'The whole army – the whole campaign plan – depends upon that damned bridge being captured.' Von Dodenburg raised his voice. 'Lads, I know I'm asking the impossible from you. But too many of your comrades have died to capture that damned bridge down there. We can't give up now. We owe it to them. Do you understand that?'

The obvious sincerity in the young officer's voice moved even the veterans. Matz nodded his head. 'Ay, you're right there, sir. Too many good lads have gone hop for that shitting bridge. But, with the Colonel's permission, how are we going to pull it off with what we've got at our disposal now?'

'I've thought about that, Matz,' von Dodenburg answered eagerly. 'There is nothing left for us but to try the old deception trick with the Sherman.'

'But that would be suicide, sir,' Schulze protested. 'A real old Ascension Day mission. Even those buck-toothed Tommies in their stupid piss-pot helmets wouldn't fall for that one now. Great crap on the Christmas Tree, sir, they know that there are only enemy troops – ourselves – on this side of the river!' He shook his big head. 'No, sir, they won't buy it, believe me. I think we—'

His words ended, as Matz gave him a sharp dig in the ribs. 'Don't listen to the big streak of yellow piss,' he said scornfully, pushing by a surprised Schulze. 'I always knew he'd cream his knickers one of these days. Sir, I volunteer to take the Sherman. Those shitty Belgies can make up the rest of the crew. Give me five minutes start. Once they tumble to who we are, I'll mask the Tommy tanks guns the best I can. Then it's up to the lads in the Tigers to rush the bridge the best they can.'

Before von Dodenburg could reply, Schulze pushed by Matz and snapped to attention, his massive chest thrust out, as if he were back on a parade ground in the Fatherland, facing the whole Wotan. 'Sir, beg permission to take charge of the Sherman,' he bellowed. 'Most experienced NCO in the whole Wotan and its senior noncom too, sir. It's my right and duty, if I may point out the regulations to you. Besides,' he added scornfully, dropping his formal tone, 'that one-legged cripple behind me wouldn't even be able to find his way down to the shitty bridge. The old shit is as blind as a bat.'

* * *

The Field Marshal was in no way offended when the young liaison officer from his 'eyes and ears' team[1] knocked at the door of his caravan and requested permission to enter. Although it was only just after six, he was wide awake and sipping his morning tea under the big portrait of Field Marshal Gerd von Rundstedt which, save for a signed picture of King George VI, was the caravan's sole decoration.

'Well,' he snapped, keen eyes sizing up the young Rifle Brigade officer's mud-stained uniform, 'what news?'

The officer wiped his wind-chapped lips and tore his longing gaze from the mug of tea. 'The Boche have appeared at the bridge at Huy, sir – as you predicted they would.'

Montgomery took the news calmly. But he gave the young officer a wintry smile of appreciation in return for the flattery. The 'Master', as he was called by his 'eyes and ears', never disdained praise, however obvious. 'Yes, I thought they would. And the situation?'

The officer pointed to the big map on the desk. 'If I could show you, sir? They came in, in – perhaps – company strength down here. They almost took our chaps by surprise. They were pretty well beat from the long drive down from Holland under these terrible conditions—'

'Did our people see the Boche off?'

'Yessir. They tumbled to the attack just in time. As far as they could tell, they about wiped out the Jerry attack company, apart from a handful of prisoners.'

'What unit?'

'Wotan – the one that made General Hodges withdraw the other day, sir.'

[1] A small team of battle-experienced officers who reported directly to Montgomery from all fronts. (*Transl.*)

Montgomery's face lit up momentarily. 'Yes, they did make our American cousin do a bit of a bunk, didn't they?' He tweaked the end of his beaky nose. 'What about armour?'

'Nothing definite, sir. But one of the prisoners – a major I believe – said they had hundreds of tanks on the heights. But he'd been very badly hit – blinded – and was rambling, according to the MO.'

The Field Marshal considered the information for a moment, the tips of his long fingers pressed together under his chin so that he looked, in the pale light of the caravan, like some ascetic Early Church Father. 'That may be so, my boy. But we can't take any risks. After all we are dealing with the Boche's elite formation. Would you please inform Freddie that he must order the brigade commander on the spot to advance across the river in force. If necessary, I'll release another tank battalion from Thirty Corps to give him any assistance he requires.'

'And his objective, sir?'

'Objective? I want what is left of Battle Group Wotan to be wiped off the face of the earth. Then perhaps I can show our American friends at Chaudfontaine how to begin tidying up a very untidy battlefield.' He smiled bleakly at the young officer. 'After all that is how I won the Second Alamein, wasn't it?'

* * *

A thin yellow sun slid over the grey winter horizon, tried to struggle higher, failed and lay there, as if exhausted or beaten by the bitter greyness of the morning.

The bridge was silent. To the left and right, the Churchills waited expectantly, buttoned down, the commanders tensely glued to their periscopes, the gunners poised over the freezing breeches of their 17-pounders. To their front the bridge was littered with the dead of the dawn battle, and the debris of war: smashed ammunition boxes, abandoned rifles, rusting wire, helmets, a severed foot complete with its boot. Here and there a head moved cautiously. But the tank commanders, as tense and anxious as the infantry dug into the shattered houses behind

[1] Presumably Major General Freddie de Guingand, Montgomery's Chief-of-Staff. (*Transl.*)

them, knew that they belonged to their own men – artillery and mortar spotters, prepared in an instant to bring a hail of fire down on any enemy intruder.

The minutes passed leadenly. Behind them in the silent medieval town on the heights, a clock began to strike the hour of eight. It broke off after the fourth stroke, as if some frightened verger or priest had stopped it lest it draw unwelcome attention to his church.

The tank commanders expelled a sigh. Despite the freezing cold inside the unheated tanks, most of them were sweating. They were old hands. They had been in the fighting since Normandy and knew the strength of the Tiger, almost impregnable as it was from the front. Why, hadn't one Tiger manned by a handful of bold SS men from the *Hitler Youth Division*, shot up a whole British tank brigade outside Caen? Their own Churchills were out-dated, ready for replacement by newer models. Indeed they had been on their way to replace them at the depots in Holland when they had been ordered to the Meuse so suddenly. Now, if the information the brigade intelligence officer had managed to drag out of the blinded, half-crazed SS Major before he had fainted was true, there were scores of Tigers up in the silent, snow-covered heights above them. Soon they would coming barrelling down from those heights – and then all hell would be let loose. Here and there the more anxious gave a quick twist of the handle on the emergency escape hatch. Once the 88s started smashing into them, there wouldn't be much time for fiddling with the winter-stiff handles.

On the roof of the eighteenth century red-brick factory overlooking the vital bridge the moustachioed Brigadier Commander was surveying the opposite bank with his binoculars, his head wreathed in a grey cloud of his own breath, when Montgomery's message was handed to him by an aide, panting from the long climb. He read it through quickly and stuffed it angrily in the pocket of his grey tank overall. 'Blast and damn it all, Charles!' he snorted.

'What is it, sir?'

'For some reason or other, Monty, in all his wisdom, wants

us to cross the river and take on the Jerries up the hill. We've got to put all our tanks across.' He sighed. 'All right, Charles, tell the chaps to start moving out.'

Charles opened his mouth to protest, but the moustachioed Brigadier stopped him before he could speak. 'I know, Charles, you don't have to signal it. The chaps are windy about those damned Tigers, but I can't help that. Just tell them to get their skates on going up that damned hill. Because if the Jerries catch them up there in single file, he'll have the balls off them as soon as winking. Now move it!'

* * *

Thus it was that Schulze's Sherman, moving cautiously down the slippery, battle-littered hill in low gear, turned a bend to be confronted by a long line of equally cautious Churchills, crossing the bridge and advancing up the incline. Schulze reacted first. There was no use trying to bluff it out. Besides the Churchills were all along the bridge, spread out at convoy distance upon it. Their mission had failed before it had properly begun.

'Churchill at two o'clock, Matz!' he yelled through the throat mike, and pushed Sepp away from the gun to press the button operating the electric turret mechanism. Smoothly and swiftly it swung to the right.

He pressed his eye to the rubber sight and grabbed for the firing lever. The first Churchill filled the round glass. The cross wires centered squarely on the joint between the deck and squat turret – its weakest spot. While the Churchill gunner was still trying to crank his long 17-pounder round by hand, Schulze fired.

The Sherman shuddered violently. A wave of hot acrid smoke flooded the compartment. Schulze coughed thickly and automatically pressed the button which operated the electric fan to clear the smoke. One hundred metres away, the Churchill was slammed up against a wall.

'You got the Tommy bastard!' Matz yelled exultantly.

'Shut up!' Schulze cried. 'Get us through that house – at ten o'clock! Quick!'

As the next Churchill opened fire, sending the whirling blob of an armour-piercing shell hurtling towards them, Matz swung the Sherman round and smashed into the nearest house. They crunched their way through what might have been a living room. A french window loomed up. Instinctively Schulze closed his eyes. With a crash of bursting glass, they were through it and churning their way through an ornamental garden, scattering snow, soil and plaster flower vases everywhere. Behind them the roof collapsed with a thunderous roar and a shower of tiles.

But Schulze had no time for the roof. He knew he would have to do some quick thinking, if he were ever to get them out of this mess. He could abandon the tank and make a run for it on foot, but Matz was too slow with his peg-leg, and besides they had caught a glimpse of Tommy infantry coming up behind the Churchills.

'That wall, Matz!' he yelled desperately. 'One o'clock! For shit's sake, man, can't you see it!'

Matz swung the tank round furiously.

'Brake!' Schulze commanded.

Now from behind the cover of the wall, they were flanking the long line of Churchills stalled by the wrecked tank at the point. Khaki-clad infantry were milling around in confusion, weapons at the ready, looking for the enemy tank which had vanished so suddenly.

'All right, Matz, this is what we're gonna do,' Schulze explained, not quite able to control his voice, while Hairless Harry loaded another 75 mm shell. 'I'm gonna let the Churchill – at that bend there – have it in the knackers. If we knock him out, we've got the road blocked. Then when I open up, Sepp here can tackle the infantry. Once the road's blocked and the Tommy stubble-hoppers are pinned down, I want you to back out. There must be a shitty parallel street going up the hill.'

'And the mission?' queried Matz.

'Forget it, we'll be lucky if we get out of this little lot without having our eggs sliced off. All right, put her into reverse. Here we go!'

He threw one final glance round the turret. Satisfied he

pressed himself against the big gun again. The Churchill stalled at the bend filled the sight. The cross-wires met just in front of its rear sprocket. Hit it and Schulze knew it would take a tank recovery vehicle to move the bastard. Schulze held his breath, feeling a cold trick of sweat moving down the small of his back. Slowly his hand began to squeeze the firing lever. Beside him Sepp tensed over the .30 calibre machine-gun.

'*Fire!*'

Again the gun erupted. The Sherman heaved like a ship at sea. Hot smoke slapped against their faces, and then Sepp's machine-gun began to chatter.

When the smoke cleared they saw that the Churchill had slumped to the right, a gaping hole where its rear sprocket had been, a trail flung out brokenly in front of it. The Tommy stubble-hoppers were running panic-strickenly for cover. Khaki-clad bodies lay in twitching heaps in the blood-red snow. A sudden madness – an exhilarating blood lust – overcame Sepp. Gasping like a man in the throes of sexual ecstasy, he swung the machine-gun from left to right, hurling a vicious hail of fire at the trapped Tommies. For a moment, Schulze forgot their position. He, too, was seized by the desire to kill. Then he caught himself in time.

'All right, Matz?' he yelled above the chatter of the machine-gun. 'Let's get the hell out of here – *quick*!'

Matz needed no urging. With an ear-splitting roar, the Sherman backed from the wall. Already lead was beginning to patter against its metal sides and flares were soaring into the sky everywhere. Matz had no eyes for them. Desperately he flung the Sherman forward. A greenhouse loomed up. He went through it in crazy shower of glass. A wall. Through it, glass flying everywhere. Down a little alley, so narrow that they could hear the rough ancient stones ripping at the steel.

'*There!*' Schulze screamed suddenly. '*To the right!*' Matz saw the little street, rising steeply, in the same instant. Instinctively he flung the Sherman to the right. It was the parallel road they were seeking. But it was also the road that led straight into the stalled column of Tommy anti-tank gunners, their six-pounders deployed and ready for action.

For a moment the Tommies were slow to react. Then a big officer in a leather jerkin with a cane in his hand recognized the looted Sherman. He screamed something. The first six-pounder spun round.

'Look out!' yelled Hairless Harry. Desperately Schulze tried to hand crank the 75 mm round. To no avail. An AP shell traced a dull red path around the outside of the turret. Horrified they watched its ruddy progress. If it penetrated the turret, they were done for. With a banshee-howl it careened off.

Schulze opened his mouth to give the order to bail out. But he found that he could not speak. 'Come on,' screamed Matz frantically, 'let's get the hell out of this coffin. We've got one thousand litres of gas on board – it'll go up at any minute!'

With the last of his strength, Schulze pulled the smoke discharger trigger.

'*Now!*' Matz yelled urgently, and the three survivors scrambled wildly out of the stricken Sherman, pelting for the cover of the nearest house, coughing harshly as the thick white smoke penetrated their bursting lungs. Behind them they could hear cries of rage in English.

'Keep ... keep ... running,' gasped Schulze. He swung round. Matz was beginning to lag far behind. 'Matz ... keep up—'

The words died on his lips for as he came to a ragged halt, his chest heaving crazily, he saw that Matz was falling, his chin thrust back, his oil-stained hands clawing the air, as if he were trying to grab handfuls of it to keep himself upright. A sudden line of dark holes had appeared along the length of his arched spine from which the blood had already begun gush.

'*MATZ!*' he screamed. '*MATZ!*'

But Matz did not hear him. His legs were beginning to buckle beneath him, the wooden one sticking out at an awkward angle.

'Matz!' he screamed again, oblivious to the slugs hissing through the smoke.

'Piss off,' the one-legged NCO cried, 'Let me croak ... in peace ...'

His words broke Schulze's horrified trance. He pelted forward, head ducked into his big shoulders like an American football player. Just as Matz's good leg gave way for good, Schulze grabbed him round the waist, the blood spurting out thickly and drenching his hands. Tugging the dying man to his hip like a mother does a heavy child, he hobbled to the house, the furious slugs, deprived of their victim, throwing angry little spurts of snow up all around his blood-covered boots.

* * *

They crouched fearfully in the icy cellar, Schulze's bloody hand still pressed over Matz's mouth, although the heavy searching boots were almost past. Very slowly he released his grip. The Tommies wouldn't find them now.

Matz's mouth was wide open, his breath coming in shallow, gasps as if he could not get enough air. His unshaven chin was thick with black-red blood. Slowly his tongue was beginning to furl back in his throat.

'He'll choke,' Sepp said in alarm.

'Give me that sabre of yours,' Schulze commanded. 'Quick!'

The Belgian fumbled for his big pocket knife. Hastily Schulze clicked it open and, thrusting it in Matz's mouth, gently clamped his teeth on it. For an instant he looked at Matz's blood-soaked grey pants. 'All right,' he said, 'I'm gonna turn him over and look at his back. I want you to hold his head up so he doesn't choke to death.'

With surprising gentleness for such a big man, he grasped Matz's shoulders and began to turn him round. Matz groaned and his eyelids flickered for a moment, didn't open.

'Oh, my Christ!' Schulze gasped when he saw the condition of Matz's lower back. 'Haemorrhage – internal haemorrhage.'

'He'll bleed to death, if we don't stop it,' Sepp hissed. Schulze nodded, his brain racing in an attempt to find some way to save his old crony and whoring partner. '*Matz!*' He took the dying NCO's head out of Sepp's hands and cradled it in his lap, the knife hanging from Matz's mouth at an angle. 'How are you?'

'Like shit,' he said, his voice hardly audible.

'You've been hit in the guts, Matzie.' Schulze said, swallowing hard and looking down at the other NCO's ashen-grey face, with great violet circles under the eyes.

'Bin . . . bin hit before in worse—' He broke off suddenly. His face seemed suddenly pinched, the nose longer than it had ever been, his eyelashes flickering like some St Pauli whore's.

Schulze knew the signs. He had seen them often enough before. 'Matz,' he cried harshly, 'open your eyes!' Schulze pressed him hard. He could feel the blood pouring down the back of his hand and running in a wild torrent up his sleeve. 'Matz – open yer shitting eyes!' He screamed. 'If you don't—'

He stopped short, for Matz's head had flopped to one side, his mouth open wide, his limbs limp.

'Matz!' Schulze screamed once more.

As the cry echoed through the abandoned cellar, Sepp gently released the dead man from Schulze's grip.

* * *

'All right, this is the drill,' von Dodenburg rapped through his throat mike, his voice unemotional, 'we're going to slog it out with them. If we can't take the bridge, then we'll at least hold the height until our troops catch up with us.' Even as he said the words, he knew that the Butcher Boy's men would never link up with them now. 'Numbers three and four will take up position to the left of the road. Number two will join me on the right.' He flashed a look at the thick black pyre of smoke rising from below. He bit his bottom lip grimly; for he knew what it signified – the Sherman had bought it. Matz, Schulze and the two front-runners were dead or prisoner. He pressed the throat mike again. 'Half-track.'

'Sir?'

'Try to raise Army HQ and let them know what our situation is, and,' he hesitated, 'if we don't get back – beat it the way we came. All right, let's roll 'em.' With a sudden metallic squeaking, the command Tiger jolted forward, followed by its number two. Von Dodenburg took one last look at them and the road.

From below the rattle of the advancing Churchills was growing louder. As he pulled down the turret hatch, he wondered if he would live to see the hill-top again. A moment later, the Tiger driver crashed the sixty-ton monster into the wall of one of the little white-washed peasant cottages. The old rickety roof collapsed at once, burying the Tiger in a rubble of dusty bricks and slates. A little further off the tank's running mate did the same and both drivers switched off their engines. In the sudden silence the waiting men could hear the grunts of the gunners as they hand-cranked their great hooded cannon round to face the road, and below, the steady clatter of the Tommy tanks as they advanced unawares into the steel trap.

The first Churchill spun round the bend at a right angle, the driver fighting furiously to keep control on the slippery slope.

'Not yet,' hissed von Dodenburg, as he felt the young gunner tense at his side in the gloom of the icy turret. 'There'll be a lot more of them to come yet.'

As the lead tank advanced at a snail's pace towards their position, its 17-pounder swinging from side to side like the snout of some primeval monster seeking out its prey, tank after tank followed in a hesitant column. Von Dodenburg could almost smell the Tommy crews' fears, waiting tense and expectant for the shells.

Von Dodenburg laid his hand carefully on the young gunner's shoulder. 'Lead tank – AP,' he said. 'One round – no more.' He leaned forward and cradled a gleaming yellow round in his arms. 'Then switch immediately to number six Churchill.'

The gunner, his face covered in a thin lather of sweat, nodded without taking his eye from the sight, following the lead tank's progress almost lovingly.

Von Dodenburg peered into his periscope. There were ten Tommy tanks on the steep slope, labouring upwards in low gear – and there were still more following them. Another one hundred metres, and the point Churchill would be round the bend and spot the half-track. It was time to act.

He pressed the throat mike. 'Listen everybody – get ready to fire. I'm taking numbers one and six. For you – targets of opportunity. Over and out!' Suddenly his voice rose harshly. He brought his hand down on the gunner's shoulder – hard. '*Fire!*'

The horizon trembled. A howling wind swept the road as the silence was torn apart. The breech shot back. A long steaming yellow cartridge case clattered to the deck of the tank and von Dodenburg rammed home the next round, flinging himself at the periscope.

'Number six,' von Dodenburg bellowed, as the other Tigers opened fire.

The sweating gunner, fighting his wheels with frantic frenzied hands, swung the long deadly cannon round, his right shoulder hunched. He grunted. Again the 88 erupted, and everything became a wild breathless chaos. On both sides of the road tanks and houses were burning. Someone was firing a machine-gun in crazy bursts of tracer. Two Churchills attempting to get out of the trap smashed together in a fiery rain of sparks. Some tank's gas tank exploded with a thick crump. A great mushroom of black smoke began to ascend to the merciless grey sky. Blackened corpses strewed the ground. And all the time the great 88 cannon smashed round after round into the trapped British.

'By the great whore of Buxtehude!' swore von Dodenburg's gunner, as if his innocent eyes had ever seen a whore, 'the Tommies are going to be slaughtered this day.'

* * *

Charles, his helmet gone, his once elegant uniform oil-stained and bloody, pushed his way carelessly through the staff officers grouped around the tank brigadier. 'Sir, sir,' he gasped, oblivious to the staff officers' disdainful looks, 'the men are being massacred there up on the hill. 'We ran into a trap.'

The Brigadier looked down at him, as if he had suddenly appeared out of the woodwork. 'I say,' he said in his most affected Sandhurst accent. 'don't you salute your senior officer when you wish to speak to him, Charles? I know we're not exactly the Guards in this brigade, but there are certain proprieties which one must observe, don't you think – even in this horrid business.' He stared shrewdly at the twenty-two-year-old Captain. He had seen this sort of thing often enough before – in France, Greece, the Desert, Normandy. Once you let it get out of hand, the panic spread to everyone – officers and other ranks – like an infectious disease.

Charles swallowed hard and gave a parody of a salute, the blood dripping down his right arm as he raised it to his bare head. 'Sir, as far as I can judge Jerry has knocked out eight of our tanks. They're sited in the houses on both sides of the height – in the hull-down position – and they've got what's left of our chaps trapped. As soon as they attempt to move out of cover, the Jerry brews them up straight away.'

The Brigadier nodded casually. 'Bad show, what? Looks as if they've got us by short and curlies, eh?' He looked at the staff officers' suddenly worried faces, and smiled suddenly. 'Not to worry, chaps. We'll manage. Charles, your chaps will put down smoke and pull out as best they can. I'll push a troop of anti-tank up the hill to try to give them some sort of cover. In the meantime, I want PIAT-men[1] up there on the double. They can infiltrate into the houses.' He threw a quick glance at the leaden sky. 'Once it starts to snow and visibility goes, they're going to take out those bloody Jerry panzers one by one, if it's the last thing I do!'

* * *

Half an hour later it started to snow hard, as the Brigadier had guessed it would. Coming in straight from the north, the fist-sized flakes had covered the dead and smouldering hulks of the shot-up Churchills in a matter of minutes. Visibility was reduced to fifty metres and the world transformed into a howling wilderness. Almost immediately the infantry piat-men, led by the moustachioed Brigadier in his beret and heavy tank overalls, started to move in for the kill.

Von Dodenburg recognized the danger at once. Red-eyed, his face black with powder and oil, his voice hoarse with smoke, he rasped, 'Driver, start up – ready to move out immediately.'

[1]A one-man anti-tank device. (*Transl.*)

Using all his strength he pushed open the hatch, the litter of brick rubble upon it slithering down on to the deck. Gratefully sucking in a great gulp of the icy air, he narrowed his eyes against the driving snow and tried to penetrate the gloom, his machine-pistol held at the ready. But he could see nothing. He could only hear the soft squelch of heavy boots across the new snow. The Tommy infantry was already out there somewhere – getting closer by the minute.

Then across the street a spurt of scarlet flame leapt skywards, illuminating the stricken number four, its right track snapped, its commander climbing painfully from the turret with blood pouring down the side of his shattered face. Then the streaming snow closed in again and cut off his vision.

'Driver,' cried von Dodenburg harshly, 'back out – now!'

Pressing his throat mike, he repeated the message to the commanders of the remaining two Tigers, spraying a wide arc to his front with lead and cursing the fact that the tracer would give away his position. And of course the Tommies spotted him at once. A mere forty metres away scarlet flame sliced the white gloom. While a dark object started to wobble towards the Tiger, gathering speed at every moment. '*Left!*' he yelled. 'On to the road.'

The Tiger lurched forward, nearly throwing von Dodenburg out of the turrent and the move took the Tommies completely by surprise. A good dozen bombs struck the Tiger's thick steel hide at an angle, ricocheting off without damage. The big tank careered to the right and began ascending the hill followed by the other two survivors, while Dodenburg, blinded by the snow, fired wild bursts into the houses on both sides.

But the Tommies were already pressing home their attack against the blinded helpless monsters grinding up the hill at less than five miles an hour.

'For Christ's sake, can't you move faster, driver?' von Dodenburg pleaded.

'I can't, sir. The shitty tracks just won't get a proper grip on the snow! A bit too much power – and the bastard will stall altogether.'

Von Dodenburg bit his lip in despair. He could make out the dark shapes slipping from door to door behind them. Even the driving snow could not obscure them – they were that close. He tugged round the turret machine-gun and poured a stream of tracer at them.

Behind them the remaining Tiger was slipping further and further to the edge of the road, its tracks flailing wildly, as the frantic driver tried to fight it back on to the centre and away from the tank-killers lurking in the dark doorways. Millimetre upon millimetre it crept towards them, while they waited like vultures for the animal which could no longer defend itself. Horrified, von Dodenburg watched as the concentrated fire of a good twenty Tommies poured at the Tiger from the closest possible range. It exploded almost at once, sending great chunks of metal and flesh flying through the snow in a macabre dance. When the smoke cleared, there was nothing left but a patch of wet melting snow and a couple of crazily spinning sprocket wheels.

Von Dodenburg saw that it would only be a matter of minutes before his tank suffered the same fate.

'Listen driver,' he yelled, spraying the Tommies who were now moving forward again, elated at their victory, 'when I say "go", I want you to swing her round and head straight for the Tommies back there—'

'*What?*'

'Don't ask questions, do as I say. Swing her round and then get ready to bail out. All right – *Go!*'

The driver spun the controls. The 60-ton monster whipped deftly round on the slick surface like a professional ice-skater showing off one of her best tricks. Thrusting home low gear, he accelerated and the Tiger started to rumble forward, gathering speed with every second.

'Get out!' von Dodenburg ordered and, grabbing his machine-pistol in both hands, dived over the side of the turret. One by one the crew followed, rolling over in the soft snow.

Twenty-five metres below them, the Tommies scattered wildly, as the great tank rolled towards them. Most of them were young men. They dodged its roaring tracks easily. Not the middle-aged Brigadier, hampered by the heavy tank overalls. The Tiger struck him a glancing blow, and knocked him beneath the right track, churning his limbs into a pulp and splattering the pieces on all sides as the metal monster rolled towards the bridge.

'Come on,' von Dodenburg gasped, pointing his Schmeisser at the crooked lane that led off from the snow-covered road, 'down here!'

'No, sir – *over here* – quick!'

He spun round, hardly believing his ears, peering through the whirling white gloom. The shouts of the pursuing Tommies were getting louder again. Already he could hear the snapping bark of their sten guns. Then the snow ceased for a fraction of a second and he caught a glance of that well-known face, grinning wearily at him, and a big hand beckoning at him and the four survivors to hurry across the road. It was Schulze with Starving Sepp, waving urgently at his side.

'My Holy Christ, you, Schulze!' he gasped.

'Who did you think, sir – Father shitting Christmas?'

* * *

They stood on the height, their chests heaving. Below them the Tommies had stopped their chase. They could hear the harsh sound of picks and shovels striking the frozen earth beneath the thick layer of snow. They were digging in, presumably to await the German attack which would never come now.

Von Dodenburg turned to look at his 'command' – exactly five men out of the five thousand who had once made up SS Battle Group Wotan. 'Schulze,' he breathed, his breath fogging around his mouth in the freezing winter air, 'what about Sergeant Matz?' Schulze shrugged. Sepp, standing trembling next to him, thrust his thumb downwards.

Von Dodenburg thrust his helmet back and wiped the red puckered, sweaty line that ran across his brow. 'All right, lads,' he began wearily, 'this is what we're going to do . . .'

High above them in the snow-heavy firs, Abe Rosenbloom had seen enough. Even at a distance of two hundred yards he had not failed to recognize the blond Kraut officer, with his black leather jacket and the gleaming decoration at his throat. Hate welled up inside him, burning the cold out of his frozen body. For a moment he raised his carbine and levelled it at the Kraut Colonel who had been responsible for the massacre of so many poor Joes at the frontier; then he lowered the weapon again. A bullet through the heart would be too clean a death for the German; he must hang by the neck at the end of a rope, with the life being squeezed out of him with excruciating pain. The bastard must suffer – and suffer some more after that. Rosenbloom started to crawl carefully up the slope to report back to VD waiting in their camp.

'Well, then Schulze,' von Dodenburg concluded, tugging down his helmet again, 'you take the lead. I'll bring up the rear. From now onwards, lads, if we're ever going to get back to our lines and the Homeland, it's going to be – march or croak. You understand that, don't you?'

The exhausted, pinched-faced young men standing shivering in the snow, shoulders hunched with exhaustion and the cold, nodded.

'All right, let's move out. It'll be dark soon now. Five metres interval between each man.'

One by one they turned and, following Schulze, started to plod wearily through the knee-deep snow like old men. For a moment von Dodenburg did not move. Instead he stared down at the little bridge so far below and so peaceful in the thin yellow rays of the setting sun.

Soon the bridge at Huy would become simply a map reference on some staff officer's map like so many other map references, marking the obscure hills, God-forsaken villages, abandoned trench lines that he had known and fought for during these last terrible five years. The chilly little number or group of black letters would never again be able to conjure up the passions or emotions of those who had fought there: the burning heat, the fierce cold, the abject cowardice, the unbelievable daring, the suffering, the fear, the exultation of those who had fought and died for those black spots on the map.

They had become history and who would ever know that on

that obscure little bridge at Huy, the Thousand Year Empire of Adolf Hitler had lost the war? Without a second look, he turned and began to plough his way after the others. He would never see the Bridge at Huy again.

6

Thursday, December 21st 1944.

Rosenbloom slithered down the steep embankment to their camp in a flurry of snow. 'VD,' he gasped, 'they've had it! What's left of the Kraut bastards are bugging out!'

VD, veteran that he was, nodded casually and did not stop fanning the fire. 'Okay, okay, don't race ya engine, Ikey. I knew they would.'

Rosenbloom flushed angrily and promised himself that one day he'd plant one on the little NCO's goddam big red nose. But if his news did not seem to have an effect on VD, it did on the other men crouched shivering in the little glade, seeking protection from the icy wind in the firs.

The medic with the broken eye-glasses dropped the can of cold hash he had been eating for breakfast and said enthusiastically. 'So they're going at last. Thank Christ for that!' He wiped his sleeve across his blue, dripping nose. 'What ya say, sarge? Perhaps we can go down to the Limey lines now.' He aimed an angry kick at the empty can. 'Gee, have I had enough of that crap – and it's cold enough to freeze the nuts off'n a goddam brass monkey!'

'Yeah, yeah, you're not goddam shitting there, Doc,' agreed several of the frozen men, standing around in the icy morning air dourly.

'We've sure had a belly-full of this crap!'

VD took his time. He hawked deliberately and then with a contemptuous puff of his cracked lips spat a gob of yellow phlegm on to the snow directly in front of the medic's boots. 'Did I hear you say something, Doc?' he asked softly and menacingly.

The medic overheard the menace. 'But Sarge, we've been out here in this goddam shit for days now, without a roof over our heads and no decent chow! Hell, we screwed the Heinies yesterday when we lit the beacon—'

His complaint ended in a gasp, as VD's dirty hand shot out and grabbed him by the neck. 'Listen buddy,' hissed the little NCO, bringing his leathery, bearded face close to the other's young, unlined one, 'what in Sam Hill do you think this goddam is? A Sunday School hayride with taffy apples and soda pop – or a goddam shooting war?'

The medic choked furiously and tried to free himself from VD's iron grip, but without success. VD thrust his face even closer to the medic's.

'Down there somewhere or other, son, there is one Kraut colonel and his sidekicks and I aim to get me that colonel.'

'Yeah, and remember, he's responsible for all them Joes buying it at the border,' Rosenbloom added. 'In goddam cold blood!'

VD nodded sagely without taking his hard little eyes off the medic's face.

'But all we've gotta do, Sarge,' another man protested, 'is to let the Limeys take care of them—'

VD spun round furiously, still holding on to the medic, now frightened into a frozen silence, 'Listen, you four-eyed bugger. This is an American war. All over the goddam Ardennes, American boys are getting hit and killed – *not* Limeys. So what does that mean, four-eyes? It's means we're gonna finish this off – we Americans. Not the limeys, do you read me, guys? Besides most of you guys was in England before we came over here. You know the Limeys. We can't rely on them. The Krauts'd be up and off even before they'd finished their breakfast muffins! No, we started this goddam thing and we're goddam gonna finish it.' He strode back to the fir and picked up his grease-gun, leaning against it, the breech carefully wrapped up in a piece of sacking he had picked up somewhere or other. 'All right, guys, grab a hold of ya weapons.' He slung the grease-gun over his shoulder. 'Come on, now let's haul ass.' He grinned pleasurably at their sullen frozen faces, as they stumbled off to fetch their weapons, plodding slowly through the deep snow. 'We're gonna go Kraut hunting.' He winked at Rosenbloom. 'What do you say, *Abe*?'

* * *

It was unearthly cold. The icy wind raced across the winter waste at eighty kilometres an hour. It lashed millions of razor-sharp snow particles against their sunken faces. Icicles hung cruelly from their nostrils and eyelashes. Every single breath was like a knife to the lungs. Their weary shoulders bent under the strain as they stumbled their way across the never-ending white plain.

Only habit and the iron discipline of the SS kept them going – that and the flickering, ever weakening desire to stay alive. With von Dodenburg at the point, Schulze – in the rear – bullied, cajoled, pleaded with the exhausted young men to keep going. Now and again, a weary trooper would close his eyes, and sink gratefully into the soft snow, to wait for death. Schulze, summoning up some last reserve of strength, would be on to him at once, kicking and slapping the protesting trooper to his feet, he would force him to stagger after the rest, more often than not carrying the trooper's weapon in addition to his own, while the wildly swaying youth sobbed at his side. But both he and a frantic von Dodenburg leading the little column knew that if they did not find shelter and food soon, it would be only a matter of hours before – one after another – they slumped wearily into the snow to die.

Sepp did not want to die. For hours now he had been keeping himself going by the delightful memory of that breakfast at Stavelot: the spluttering eggs frying; the mounds of white bread; the bubbling urns of deliciously hot coffee. His eyes closed against the howling icy wind, his stomach rumbling furiously, that glorious breakfast, which had caused the death of so many of Harsch's young grenadiers, drew him on and on like an enormous magnet.

Suddenly Sepp's nostrils twitched. Even at this stage of exhaustion, they did not fail him. He stumbled to a halt and opened his eyes carefully. A myriad, glass-sharp snow particles stung them painfully, but he forced himself to keep them open.

Raising his head to the wind, he sniffed the keen air. There was no mistaking it. Somewhere, someone was cooking food! Two thin streams of saliva began to run down the sides of his skinny bearded chin in anticipation. His stomach did a back-flip and he swayed dangerously.

He surveyed the white waste minutely, covering every depression, every snowy hillock, every patch of firs until he spotted it. A thin stream of blue smoke being driven furiously to the west by the bitter wind, but unmistakable all the same. He opened his mouth to shout at the others, already a hundred metres ahead of him. But he caught himself in time.

Who could be cooking out there in the shelter of the firs? There were neither Amis nor Boche out here. Obviously it was some peasant or other: one of his own Walloon compatriots, cut off by the sudden German offensive, frying the last of his eggs, perhaps with a bit of the local smoked ham – perhaps even with a piece of bread! The very thought set his hungry stomach off into a series of furious rumbles. But if he told the others, what might he get out of it? Nothing, more than likely. A sniff at the pan at the most. His eyes narrowed cunningly. No, he wouldn't tell them. He had his carbine and the peasant would be unarmed. He would take it for himself, eat it and follow the rest without their even knowing that he had fortified himself with food.

He lagged further and further behind. Schulze, preoccupied with another trooper who had just collapsed in the snow, did not notice him. It was the opportunity Starving Sepp had been waiting for. With a sudden burst of fresh energy, he began to plough through the deep snow to the bunch of firs behind which the peasant was sheltering from the wind.

But despite his overwhelming hunger, Starving Sepp was no fool. He approached the firs cautiously with his rifle clasped to his hip, taking care not to make any noise in the soft snow. Taking a deep breath, he moved a firbranch aside, ducking swiftly as the suddenly disturbed snow showered down, and sprang into the glade, his rifle at the ready.

'*You!*' he gasped.

At the little fire, the one-eyed SS sergeant stared up at him in apparent surprise. 'Sepp!' he cried. He dropped the fork into the ashes.

'But I thought you were – er – dead, Sergeant Ochmann,' the Belgian renegade said and then his eyes fell on the can of hash, bubbling seductively over the fire. 'Ami,' he breathed, 'I can smell it from here! But where in three devils' name, did you get it from—'

The sudden hard jab of a grease-gun's muzzle into the small of his back answered that question for him. 'Okay, buddy,' rasped a harsh voice. 'Freeze the mitts in the air!'

Sepp did not understand the words, but he understood their meaning well enough. His skinny arms shot into the air, his rifle falling to the snow with a soft plop. Swift hands frisked his ragged clothes.

'Okay, Sarge,' someone said. 'The Kraut's clean.' VD pushed past the soldier and gave the prisoner a quick glance.

'Okay, Kraut,' he said to Ochmann. 'That little trick saved your dirty Heinie neck for another day.'

The SS sergeant sprang to his feet, dropping the can carelessly into the fire. 'Thank you, sir ... thank you, sir. I can assure you that—'

'Knock it off, Kraut!' With his free hand VD pushed the SS sergeant in the face and sent him staggering back against one of the firs. 'You give me the goddam creeps.'

Curiously the Americans gathered around their skinny prisoner, standing there shivering, his eyes fixed on the meat from the hash can rapidly blackening in the embers, pursing his lips as if he wished he could savour the food.

'What we gonna do with the bastard, Sarge?' asked Rosenbloom.

'Do you recognize him?' VD queried. 'Was he there – at the frontier?'

Rosenbloom nodded, his dark Jewish face suddenly grim. 'Yeah, he was with the big wheel, the Nazi Colonel.'

VD stared at the snowy ground at his feet. 'One of them, eh,' he said slowly, while the little bunch of GIs watched him curiously. 'Thanks Abe.'

There was no sound now save for the howl of the winter

wind, the slither of the snow it brought down from the fir branches and the chatter of Starving Sepp's teeth, as he stared in frightened bewilderment at the foreign faces all around him, not understanding a word they said.

'But Sarge, for crying out loud, make up ya mind what ya gonna do with him,' the medic cried plaintively. 'My nuts are goddam freezing up standing here, not moving.'

VD looked up suddenly. 'Okay, Doc, I've made up my mind.'

'Yeah?'

'Yeah. We're gonna kill the bastard. To be more exact, *you're* gonna kill the bastard.'

'*What?*' the medic exploded, his pale face suddenly flooding with colour.

'And because we don't want to alarm his buddies – after all they've still got a couple of grease-guns among them – you're not gonna to be able to use your rifle.'

By way of an answer, the little bandy-legged NCO reached in his back pocket and pulled out a large clasp-knife. With his right thumb-nail, he flicked it open to reveal a wicked, razor-sharp blade. 'With this,' he said. 'Won't make a sound. Here, take it Doc. After all you're the best guy for the job – you're a trained medic, ain't ya?'

'Jesus, Sarge,' the medic breathed. 'Have a goddam heart. I never done nuthin' like this before—' The words froze on his lips as the little NCO raised his weapon and said softly. 'It's either you or him, big-mouth – so what's it gonna be?'

Starving Sepp had not understood a word of the conversation. But the appearance of knife sufficed. Gasping wildly, his eyes revolving around at their hard tense faces, he dropped on to his knees, his hands raised up to them in a babbling incomprehensible plea for mercy. But no one heeded him. While iron hands seized him on all sides, the medic, his eyes wide and staring behind his GI glasses, advance upon him, as if in a trance, the knife concealed behind his back like a dentist hiding his forceps from a frightened child. Suddenly he thrust out his free hand and seized the Belgian's skinny throat. His babbling cries for mercy ended as he sought for breath, his bulging eyes alone capable of expressing his fear and outrage.

'Get on with it, *big mouth*,' VD urged, still not lowering his weapon, which was pointed straight at the medic's heart.

Retching, the GI plunged the knife into Sepp's breast. The blood spurted out in a scarlet stream and drenched his hand. Sobbing, the bloody knife still clasped in his red hand, he hung on to the nearest tree, while Starving Sepp's body slid slowly to the ground, coming to rest with the lacerated head on the burned, charred hash, so that it looked as if, even in death, the little Belgian was stuffing food into his wide open mouth.

Coldly VD lowered his rifle. 'Okay, you guys,' he announced, his voice completely without emotion. 'The show's over. One down and five still to go. So come, on, let's get on the stick.'

Wordlessly they filed past the dead front-runner, following the little bandy-legged NCO in the hunt for the survivors of SS Assault Group Wotan. Behind them Sepp's body began to stiffen in the freezing wind.

* * *

Below them in the valley, awesome and brooding, death and destruction stretched the length of the road and disappeared around the far bend. Scattered trucks, burnt and twisted Tigers, wrecked half-tracks, mercifully covered by the snow, but still recognizable for what they once had been.

Schulze, standing bent-shouldered on the height next to von Dodenburg, broke the heavy silence. 'Do you know where we are, sir?' he asked hoarsely.

Von Dodenburg did not take his eyes off the ghastly tableau of bodies heaped indiscriminately together, a frozen hand, a bloody stump, a pair of eyes staring up accusingly from a waxen head that broke the surface of the new snow. 'No,' he said tonelessly. 'Where?'

'Back where the Amis hit the column that day – you remember?'

It seemed to take the weary young officer an age to absorb

the information; then he nodded, his frozen blue face emotionless. 'I remember.'

Schulze licked his cracked lips. 'There might . . . might be some grub down there, sir.' He hesitated. 'I'm so hungry, I could eat fried chicken shit at the moment – and enjoy it.'

'But—'

'I know, sir, it would mean robbing our own dead.' His voice grew in strength. 'But look at the rest of the lads, sir.' He waved a big hand, the knuckles white and split with frostbite, at the others standing on the height in a trancelike silence.' If they don't get something in their ribs soon and a bit of warmth, that lot of asparagus Tarzans'll be dead before the day's out.'

Von Dodenburg pulled himself together. 'You're right, Schulze – of course, you are. Come on, let's get down this slope and see what we can find.' Together, while the other three men slumped down gratefully into the snow, as if it were a warm, feather-bed, the two old comrades, the only survivors now of the original Wotan Battalion, started to slither down the steep slope, waist-high in loose snow.

Grimly they commenced the ghastly business of searching the wrecked vehicles and the bodies of the men in them for the life-saving food they needed so desperately now. A wrecked Tiger, its crew now a black putrid paste on its fire-red inner walls, the only trace of their existence a few charred bones. A half-track driver, his guts ripped open, the viscera swelling out of the hole like a giant sea-anemone. A truckload of panzer grenadiers, already turned black, sitting upright in their seats like rotting cabbage stumps in some winter-abandoned allotment. A group of infantry about to set up a machine-gun in a ditch and caught there by the sudden bombs, their moment of devotion to duty expressed in the passionate eloquence of their dramatic postures.

Von Dodenburg could go on no more. While Schulze – his teeth clenched tightly together to prevent himself from retching – continued to search the evil-smelling bodies, the young CO straightened up, sudden tears of both rage and compassion in his weary, blood-shot eyes.

So many men, he told himself, so many young men dead, who

had never really lived, perhaps never even had a woman. And dead for nothing. Then the whole damned miserable operation had been doomed to failure right from the very start. Kraemer had known it, and he had too. But what had he done to stop it? He clenched his frozen fists in angry despair. What had he ever done to stop such similar operations over these last five years? He had allowed the cream of Germany's youth to sacrifice themselves for hopeless causes. Belgium, Russia, Italy, France, now Belgium again. Death's greedy maws had opened and consumed them by their scores, their hundreds, their thousands; and they had gone willingly to their death, as if they could not wait to sacrifice their lives for the Führer, the Greater Glory of the Fatherland, SS Battle Group Wotan.

He broke off suddenly, for the young panzer grenadiers' sightless eyes seemed to stare at him in bitter reproach, as if now in death they had finally realized just how much he – and other officers like him all over Germany and on every front – had betrayed them into dying so purposelessly in this barren Belgian valley, far away from all they had ever known and loved. *Traitor . . . traitor*, their blank eyes accused him wherever he looked. He thrust up his hands in front of his eyes to ward off their looks. It was at that moment that the single rifle shot rang out. Von Dodenburg flashed a startled look upwards. For a moment nothing seemed to happen, as the echo rolled along the length of the valley. One of the three men on the height screamed, clapped his hand to his chest and came rolling down the steep slope in a furious ball of snow.

The scream acted as a signal. Flame etched an angry pattern in the grey gloom along the height. One of the survivors raised his machine-pistol, but a burst of lead caught him in the back.

'Look out, sir!' Schulze yelled frantically.

Von Dodenburg awoke to his danger as an egg grenade came sailing downwards. He flung himself in the snow and the grenade exploded with a harsh crash. Red hot splinters hissed through the air and pattered down on his helmet. Next to him Schulze raised his head, spluttering, from the snow, and fired a wild burst at the dark line of men coming cautiously over the brow of the hill. A couple went down, clutching their wounds and the rest hesitated. Someone shouted a coarse, angry order.

With a violent hiss like a redhot poker being plunged into a bowl of water, lead began to strike the snow all around them, forcing them to keep their heads down.

Schulze squirmed closer to his CO. 'Sir,' he gasped, snow sticking to his big face everywhere, 'we've got to make tracks – quick! A couple more minutes of this, and we're goners!'

'Yes, I know.' Desperately von Dodenburg sought for a way out of the trap, while bullets showered them with snow, as if death were already tracing his icy fingers across their frightened faces. Above them the cries were drawing nearer by the second.

'All right, Schulze, we've got to risk it. See that Tiger?'

'Yes.'

'Once we get that far, we can hop from one vehicle to another. Soon as we get round the bend, run hell-for-leather for the woods to the right. If I get hit, don't stop. Do you understand?'

'Yes sir. The same goes for me, sir!'

'All right. *Now!*'

As they had been trained to do so long before, the two veterans rolled once, twice, three times to the right, leaving the bullets to strike the snow harmlessly behind them. Then they were up, charging towards the Tiger, zig-zagging wildly from side to side, as the Amis were suddenly alerted to the fact that their victims were trying to escape and changed the direction of their fire.

'Heaven, arse and twine!' Schulze panted as he careened into the side of the Tiger and pressed himself against its thick protective armour, 'we've made it!'

Von Dodenburg, his chest heaving wildly, nodded. But there was no time to lose. The Amis were coming down the hill – he could hear them cursing angrily as they stumbled and fell in the deep snow – and already lead was beginning to whine off the Tiger's glacis plate. 'Come on, Schulze – on your knees. We crawl from here!'

He dropped to his knees and, clasping his machine-pistol across his breast, began to edge his way to the protection of the next vehicle. His hand slipped on something just underneath the snow. His nostrils filled with the sickly-sweet stench of a corpse and he retched. Behind him, Schulze, grunting heavily, was following his example, while slugs hissed through the air just above his big head. Suddenly he found he was sweating with fear.

They reached the safety of the shattered half-track with its silent cargo of waxen-faced dead men. But there was no stopping, for the bullets pursued them like angry wasps. They crawled on and on past vehicle after vehicle. The bend and safety were just in sight when a round Ami helmet appeared in front of Schulze. The big Hamburger flung himself forward in a tremendous leap from the crouched position. He and the Ami went down together in a confused, writhing ball of flailing arms and legs. Crazied with fear and frustration, Schulze seized the Ami by both ears and smashed his helmeted head against the side of a half-track, until the Ami's eyes rolled upwards in their death agony and thick red blood poured from his ears and nose.

'Over here – the bastards are over here, Sarge!' yelled an angry young voice to their left. Von Dodenburg fired instinctively. A grenade rolled into the snow next to him, lying there black and deadly for what seemed an age. Sobbing and trembling from head to toe, von Dodenburg seized it and hurled it at their pursuers.

The bend was only a hundred metres away now. But the Amis were also getting closer. They were obviously down the slope now, trying to infiltrate the wrecked vehicles and bullets were striking their armour from all directions. Von Dodenburg realized that he could only profit from the confused fire-fight. He flung a glance behind him at Schulze who was still there, his big face crimson with effort. 'Balls to this, you rogue,' he yelled. 'Come on, let's run for it!'

'Right, sir!' Schulze cried almost joyfully. 'I wasn't intended to crawl on all fours like a shitty-tailed infant!' He gripped his machine-pistol more firmly in his hamlike hands. 'Ready when you are, sir!'

'Then – *now*!'

They rose as one. A furious hail of bullets opened up. Lead ricocheted off the vehicles on all sides. Somewhere an Ami screamed. He had been struck by their own bullets. A round Ami helmet appeared behind a truck. Von Dodenburg fired from the hip as he ran and the helmet disappeared. A burst of fire caught his left boot, ripping off the sole and sending him sprawling full length and the machine-pistol flying from his nerveless hands.

'Are you all right—'

'Go on, for God's sake!' Von Dodenburg cut in angrily, rising to his feet. 'Go on!'

The bend was a mere twenty metres away. As if they could sense that their intended victims would soon escape, the Amis intensified their fire. Something struck Schulze in the calf of his left leg and he stopped instinctively. The action saved his life. From only ten metres away blue-yellow flame spat vicously from a bush. Screaming with pain, Schulze pressed the trigger of his Schmeisser. The machine-pistol trembled in his big hands. Snow flew in all directions and an Ami came tumbling from behind the bush, Schulze pressed his trigger again but nothing happened. His magazine was empty. With a curse, he flung the little weapon at the dying Ami, and limped on after Von Dodenburg, both of them now unarmed.

Von Dodenburg flung himself round the bend – and stopped dead. A bandy-legged Ami armed with a carbine was standing there calmly, blocking the track. He was smiling, as if he had expected this meeting all along.

His cunning eyes immediately took in the fact that von Dodenburg was unarmed. Easily he shifted the unlit stump of cigar from one side of his tough mouth to the other and said: 'Okay, Kraut, this is the end of the road for you—'

He never finished the words. In that same instant, Schulze hurtled round the bend and without pausing threw himself at the American. VD was bowled over and a wild burst of fire chattered into the sky. Schulze gave him a quick chop to the throat and closed with him. They tumbled to the snow, while von Dodenburg swayed dangerously on his feet, wondering what he should do.

VD was no match for the Hamburg ex-docker. But he was tough and agile. Twice Schulze tried to get his hands round the Ami's throat to finish him, and twice he escaped from Schulze's grasp. Once Schulze thought he had him, as they rolled back and forth in the snow, but in the last instant VD spat the stump of his cigar directly into the German's face. Then Schulze remembered an old trick from his waterfront days and suddenly released his hold. VD fell forwards. In that same moment, Schulze butted him full in the chin with his head. VD screamed. His head shot back and Schulze heard the dry crack of his spine breaking. His tough body went limp. The little Ami NCO slumped into the snow, unconscious.

Groggily Schulze staggered to his feet, bleeding now from his leg and nose. 'Crap on the Christmas Tree,' he gasped, the thick red-black blood pouring down his bearded chin unheeded. 'I . . . I . . . thought the little bastard was never . . . going to die.'

'Save your breath, Schulze,' said von Dodenburg, grabbing hold of him. 'Come on – we're nearly there now.' With von Dodenburg supporting his heavy bulk, the two of them limped on towards the woods and safety, but the CO watched the blood dripping from the big man's wounds into the snow with growing alarm.

Behind them the hoarse cries of the enraged survivors of the ambush grew fainter and fainter. It was clear enough that they had given up the pursuit. Yet von Dodenburg did not trust the sudden silence. Both of them were exhausted, unarmed and for all he knew, Schulze might be badly wounded in the leg. They had to get under cover as soon as possible before some one rallied the disheartened Amis and set them off again, tracking the escapees easily by means of the bloody trail.

The snow-bound firs loomed larger and larger in the grey afternoon gloom. He could make out a trail – perhaps some prewar fire-break – quite easily now. He tugged at Schulze's dead weight and grunted through his clenched teeth. 'Come on, Schulze. Don't give up now . . . We've nearly ditched the bastards.'

'Don't worry about them, sir,' Schulze breathed with a trace of his old spirit. 'Let the bastards come within farting distance and I'll give them a blast of the old fart-cannon – that'll finish 'em off for good.'

'That's the spirit, Schulze . . . a matter of metres now,' he urged. 'It's march or croak!' He flashed an anxious look at Schulze's pale bloody face. 'Remember that old Wotan motto? How long ago that was, eh?'

Schulze nodded, suddenly not trusting himself to speak; knowing that if he did, he would scream out loud with the burning pain in his leg. Staggering wildly from side to side, the two figures stumbled towards the firs, their exhausted faces strained and set in grim purpose, forcing their pain-racked bodies onwards by a sheer effort of will.

And then at last, they broke into the woods. A snow-heavy branch whipped forward and slashed von Dodenburg's face, as if it wished to bar their progress. The young officer did not even notice the sudden pain but blundered on, dragging the half-conscious Schulze with him, his breath escaping in wheezing gulps from his tortured lungs.

'Nearly . . . nearly,' he choked. 'One more pace, Schulze . . . one more pace . . .' Then at last. 'All right, Schulze, end . . . end of the line.'

'Hope they have . . . a nice hot waiting room,' Schulze answered faintly as he sank to the snow. 'With schnapps and . . . and hot saus—' His tough body bent in defeat at last and he fainted. Senior Sergeant Schulze, the last surviving NCO of SS Battle-Group Wotan, had arrived at the end of the road. His war was over.

Von Dodenburg stared down at him in horror. What was he to do with Schulze? He was exhausted himself, and even if he had not been, he would not have been able to manage Schulze's bulk. Slowly and painfully he bent and began to scrape snow over Schulze's form, forcing his frozen fingers to scoop up the icy mass. That finished, be broke off a fir branch. It snapped with a crack like a rifle shot. If there were any Amis lurking in the forest, they would have heard that all right. But he couldn't do anything about the noise. He broke off another couple of branches and spread them over the snow that now covered

Schulze's unconscious form. Satisfied that Schulze was hidden from any casual observer and that the snow-and-fir cover would at least retain his body heat, he turned and took his bearings. The German lines to the east couldn't be more than a couple of kilometres away. If he could dodge any stray Amis and break through, the comradeship of the SS Army would ensure that whoever the local commander was, he would send out a patrol to bring in the wounded comrade. Breaking off another fir branch, he began brushing it across the snow, sweeping away the traces of blood and their footprints and working his way towards the east until he was satisfied that Schulze's body was protected against immediate discovery. Then he turned and started to plough through the knee-deep glistening snow towards the sound of the guns.

Five minutes later, he emerged into a grey-green forest clearing and stopped dead. A heavy-set man was standing there, machine-pistol in his hands, waiting for him. For what appeared an age, they faced each other, frozen into immobility. Then Colonel von Dodenburg let his shoulders sag in defeat. Slowly he started to raise his hands in token of surrender.

'You, you,' the cry came from deep within the Ami's belly, 'low, animal.'

'*No*,' the German screamed, throwing up his hands in a pathetic attempt to protect his defenceless body.

Sergeant Abraham Rosenbloom jerked the trigger of his grease-gun. Violently it erupted in his big cook's hands. The vicious stream of slugs struck von Dodenburg at point-blank range and whirled him round and round in a terrible dance of death.

Bone splintered. Blood splattered on to the snow in ugly red gobs. The urine of fear and shock flooded von Dodenburg's slacks, as his screams reached their terrifying crescendo and his bullet-riddled body was thrown helplessly against the nearest tree. Then the firing stopped. His body started to slide down the tree trunk and he felt he was falling into an abyss, from which there would no further escape. Through the thick red mess, the Jewish God of Wrath loomed into sight, quivering as if it were the reflection in a lake. Von Dodenburg's nostrils were assailed by the smell of grease and stale cooking. He opened his mouth to plead for mercy. But no sound came. The dark swarthy face blotted out everything. It seemed to fill the whole world. Von Dodenburg summoned up the last of his strength, the blood streaming from his multiple wounds, his strength ebbing by the second.

'*Please*,' he croaked hoarsely, '*please*—' It was then that the Sergeant hawked and spat venomously into his bloody face. With the Jewish ex-short order cook's spittle dripping down his cheek, Colonel Kuno von Dodenburg, the last commander of SS Assault Battle Group Wotan, lost consciousness.

THREE: THE END OF THE ROAD

'No, my dear Colonel von Dodenburg, you're not going to get away with it as easy as that. A bullet is too good for you. No, you'll stand your trial and die at the end of rope like the rotten criminal trash you are.'

U.S. Colonel Childers to Kuno von Dodenburg, February 1946.

I

It was two o'clock on the morning of December 6th 1945. In the dark, hushed room under the barracks, the portable scaffold, made of good Vermont pine and stamped USQMC[1] was already waiting for its last victim. The twenty officials and authorized spectators who were to watch the execution were already lining the three walls, waiting for the victim to be brought in.

Colonel Homer B Childers, the Camp Commandant, whose breath still stank of the ten double whiskies he had drunk the night before in the Dachau Officers Club, looked at his wrist-watch, then cleared his throat. 'Gentlemen, may I have your attention?' His voice echoed hollowly in the dark underground room.

Their eyes swivelled around to him, some eager, some anxious, some plain scared.

'I will now allot you to your official places for the execution,' Colonel Childers said the words without any emotion; but then he had said them often enough in these last seven months since Germany had lost the war and the victors had begun to take their revenge. 'The official witnesses from the Judge Advocate's Branch will stand over here – on the southern edge of the trap door.'

The officers in question shuffled forward hesitantly, and he said, 'Not closer than five paces, gentlemen, or you might be going on a sudden one-way journey with the little Kraut bugger.'

Swiftly the Colonel grouped them around the scaffold: medical officers, four paces from the northern edge of the trap-door; military observers from the units which had fought against the Hitler Youth Division in France, seven paces from its western edge; the representative of Ike's HQ on its eastern

[1] US Quartermaster Corps. (*Transl.*)

edge, again at seven paces. It wouldn't do to have the Supreme Commander's rep pissed on when the dying man evacuated his bowels in the final agony, as they often did.

Finally the Colonel nodded to the PFC standing at the door. The PFC crooked his forefinger and beckoned to someone further up the corridor. There was the sound of heavy boots, advancing down the long dark passage in slow ritual. Colonel Childers snapped '*Attention!*' The officers and officials stiffened, their eyes fixed expectantly on the open door.

The heavy tread came closer and closer. The expectant observers could make out the soft Latin mumble of the prison's chaplain and they tensed. Then the little procession came into view: the Chaplain, his sickly Italianate face bowed over his prayer book; Master Sergeant Ed Bull, his massive frame dwarfing the rest, big hand held expectantly over his ·45; Wood, the executioner; and the prisoner, his hands tied behind his back, his gait awkward and constrained because of the braceboard which Wood had fixed to his shoulders. But in spite of his awkwardness and the violent trembling of his lower lip, there was no mistaking the message of scorn and hostility in the ashen-faced eighteen-year-old SS man's eyes as he stared at the well-fed Ami officers waiting to see him die on this damp December morning.

Colonel Childers read the young prisoner the specifications of his trial and the order directing his execution.

'SS Lieutenant Goetz, do you have a statement to make to me before the order directing your execution is carried out?' he asked finally. The young SS man from the Hitler Youth Division ran his eyes contemptuously across the Colonel's double-chinned face, across his fat chest bare of any combat direction, and shook his head slowly. Childers flushed. He looked at the Chaplain.

'SS Lieutenant Goetz,' the Chaplain asked in a barely audible voice, 'do you have anything to say to me as chaplain?'

Goetz smiled. 'When did you last visit the five-fingered widow, priest?' he replied in good English.

The little Chaplain dropped his gaze quickly and behind the

prisoner, Master Sergeant Bull, whose helmet seemed two sizes too small for his massive cropped head, clenched his hamlike fists. The Chaplain intoned a prayer. He hardly finished 'May God rest his soul', when Wood pushed in front of him, slipped round the prisoner's back and in a neat, experienced movement whipped the black hood over the German's head. The SS man tried to struggle. But Bull's hand descended upon his skinny undernourished shoulder and brought his struggles to a sudden end. Wood nodded his appreciation. Deftly he lowered the noose around Goetz's neck and tightened it just over his left ear as prescribed in Army Regulation 633–15.

The spectators tensed. Childers waited. He had come to enjoy this moment: it had the same power and suspense about it as when Trudi, his German girl-friend, bent her blonde head down on his belly and did that which gave him most pleasure in this life – save eating. Then he nodded to Wood.

Wood threw the wooden handle of the operating machinery expertly. The trap door clicked open. In a flash the prisoner was flung through it, not even touching its sides. Suddenly something bulged in the front of his shabby grey slacks. The shocked observers saw the tell-tale stain spread and spread. Then the body hung there suspended in an awesome, even frightened silence.

Colonel Childers had seen it all before, even to that last frustrated young man's attempt to propagate his own seed and was unmoved. 'Parade – rest!' he ordered.

There was an uneasy shuffle. Childers looked at his watch. The prescribed amount of time had elapsed.

'All right,' he commanded, 'medical officers make your examination!' It was a matter of routine. Master Sergeant Wood, the US Army of Occupation's Chief Executioner, had never bungled a hanging in his whole professional career; nevertheless they went through with the act, finally reporting stiffly to Childers: 'Sir, we pronounce this man officially dead.'

Childers looked at his watch to check the time. It was zero two twenty hours precisely. His official duties for this morning were over. In the morning he would write the duty report for

US Army Headquarters in Frankfurt and end it with the usual formula: 'Each official performed his task in a highly efficient manner . . . The proceedings were conducted with dignity, solemnity and military precision.' Now, before he went to Trudi, he fancied a drink.

'Gentlemen,' he said, smiling suddenly. 'I think that's that. I wonder if I could invite you all upstairs for a nightcap – or whatever you call a drink at this unholy hour?'

There was a murmur of approval from the observers. 'A damn good idea,' somebody said. 'This place is colder than a well-digger's ass, Colonel!'

Colonel Childers beamed. 'It's all right for you, you're only visitors. I've been doing it for months with these fellers from the Hitler Youth – and tomorrow we start on the Wotan.'

There were faint whistles of interest on all sides.

Childers nodded, almost proudly. 'Yeah, you heard me, gentlemen. Tomorrow, we start to get the truth out of those bastards who killed our poor boys up in the Ardennes last year. Now come on, let's get out of here.'

As they went out, Master Sergeant Bull, his face red with anger, dug the dead man in the ribs viciously. 'Wise guy,' he snarled. 'But what good has it done you now, Kraut, eh?'

* * *

The convoy of khaki-coloured two-and-half ton trucks attracted little attention in the little Bavarian town, as they ground their way up the cobbled slippery hill towards the camp. In the last six months, the shabby beaten civilians had seen enough of the Amis; all that interested them about their new masters was what they had to sell on the black market. Slowly the trucks, containing the survivors of the Wotan, rolled by the ruined skeletons of the bombed houses towards the camp and came to a halt in front of the great main door.

It was a forbidding place. Everything about it seemed grey. The high stone walls were grey. The main door was grey, save for the flaming sword shield which decorated it. The bars across the windows of the cells were grey. A grey place in a grey month in a grey year.

The officer in charge of the convoy pressed the bell. Words were exchanged through the grille in the gate. A moment passed. Then with a rusty screech the great door started to creak open to release the unmistakable odour of male sweat, boiled cabbage and despair. The convoy started to drive into the cobbled dirty courtyard while high above, the inmates craned their necks and tried to peer through their barred cell windows at the 'new boys'. For the arrival of new prisoners was an event: something which would break the dreary routine of thin soup, long exhausting hours of solitary confinement and the midnight beatings, which Master Sergeant Bull was wont euphemistically to call 'interrogations'.

The trucks stopped once more and the gate of the 'interrogation center' closed behind the convoy. Inside the darkened trucks, the men of Wotan waited for the old, old command. After all they had heard it enough in the last few terrible months since they had been picked out of Allied POW camps all over Germany by the hard-faced investigators of the American CIC. Then it came in a thick, beery slurred command: 'All right, youse guys, let's haul ass! Come on now, let's go!'

Almost instantly the tailboards were flung open, the canvas covers unwrapped and they were dropping stiffly and blinking in the sudden light to face Master Sergeant Bull and what he liked to call to his cronies in the Top Four Graders' Club down in the town 'my little ole welcoming party': a double line of brawny GI guards, each man his sleeves rolled up, despite the cold, and a pick-handle grasped in his big hand. Slowly, the American NCO marched down the stone steps and faced the ragged line of skinny, dirty ex-SS men. He paused on the last step so that he towered above even the tallest of the ex-elite of the National Socialist State.

'So you are the Wotan?' he said in a low, reflective voice, tapping his pick-handle against the side of his big muscular leg. 'You are the guys who were the best Hitler could produce.' He sniggered and winked at the expectant double line of guards. 'Hitler's elite – hell, a bunch of cripples, that's what you are! One good fart and I could blow the goddam lot of you over!'

He waited until his guards had finished laughing at his own comment. Then his face grew dark and threatening. 'And which of you Kraut bastards is *Colonel von Dodenburg?*'

Bull did not notice the sudden stiffening in the shabby ranks of the Wotan. 'Well, come on, I ain't got all goddam day! Where the hell are yer, Dodenburg?' he yelled.

A tall thin man with white-blond hair, his paralysed left hand hanging limply at his side, hobbed slowly out of the German ranks, his emaciated body trembling in the icy cold. He halted and came to a parody of the attention position in front of the massive NCO.

Bull looked at him in mock incredulity: 'You're ... you're Colonel von Dodenburg, the last commander of the Wotan?'

Von Dodenburg nodded, trying to control the trembling of his bullet-shattered body.

Bull raised his voice. 'Did you hear that, guys? This here skinny prick is the Kraut you read about in the *Stripes*[1]. The Nazi bogey man! Christ on a crutch, I could push him over with one little pinkie.' He extended his little finger in an affected manner and laughed thickly. 'Okay, buddy, get back into the ranks – and make it snappy!'

Von Dodenburg shuffled back into his place to be supported by a couple of hefty young giants with looks of adoration in their eyes. The smile disappeared from Bull's face. 'Okay, you Kraut bastards – start moving inside!' he yelled. Hesitantly the shabby prisoners began to approach the double line of guards waiting for them, pick-handles tensed. As the first man came level with them, a red-haired GI raised his foot and kicked the SS man deliberately. He stumbled and fell against the man opposite. One of the guards raised his pick-handle and brought it down on the SS man's bare head. '*No,*' screamed the German soldier as the beating started. Panic broke out.

'*Standfast!*' a well-remembered voice rasped with a little of that old authority. '*Wotan standfast!*'

The SS men froze, the old habit of iron discipline reasserting itself despite the pick-handles thrashing their defenceless bodies. Von Dodenburg hobbled through their ranks, the two

[1] US Army newspaper *Stars and Stripes*. (*Transl.*)

giants on either side. Placing himself at the head of the column, he ordered. '*SS Wotan – forward!*'

* * *

But Colonel von Dodenburg and the young men of Wotan were not prepared for the methods the Amis used to break them down and discover who was responsible for the frontier massacre the year before. They were simple but effective: separate individual prisoners from their comrades, terrorize them physically and mentally until they would have betrayed their own mothers in return for five minutes' respite from punishment.

A man is led into an underground room. His hood is removed and suddenly he is blinking into a bright light, which hides his interrogators who are seated at a long table draped with a black cloth and a crucifix: both symbol and warning. The light begins to move. For an instant it rests on the noose dangling from a beam in the ceiling before moving on to the door, which opens to admit the 'priest' in his ankle-length black robe, his hands held piously in front of his stomach. The interrogation can begin: the stage is set.

'So you're the officer who led the First Company, Panzer Grenadiers?' the sinister voice says from the darkness of the table in perfect German. 'We have been waiting to speak to you, for we know that you shot down our men without mercy.'

At his side, the 'priest' raises his head and looks at the young officer with black reproachful eyes.

'I don't know what you're talking about!' the automatic protest comes back.

'They all say that, SS man,' the voice sneers. 'But a democracy like America is not interested in taking the life of a misguided young man like you. We want the name of the man who gave the command to shoot our people – that's all. Tell us that and we'll save your neck from the gallows. There'll be food, cigarettes. We might even be able to fix you up with a woman. I bet it's a long, long time since you had a piece of ass, eh?' the voice says insidiously. 'Now come on, SS man, *sing*!'

* * *

Bull and a couple of the guards threw him on the floor and began kicking him in the ribs with systematic, harsh-gasping cruelty until at last he had to vomit blood and they stopped.

'Okay,' Bull sobbed, fighting for breath, 'now goddam lick up that vomit!'

The interpreter put his words into German and added a vicious kick to the ribs of his own to emphasize the command. The young corporal started to lick up his own vomit.

Finally Bull was satisfied the prisoner was ripe for interrogation. 'Okay Kraut,' he bellowed, 'now let's start asking a couple of questions – *and answering them*, if you know what's good for you. Number one – when did Colonel von crappy Dodenburg order you guys to start shooting at our men?'

When he wouldn't answer Bull broke first his ring-finger and five minutes later his middle finger, grunting a little with the effort of snapping back the bones. Then the prisoner fainted.

He came to, to find the Ami MO staring down at him. 'Slipped on the landing floor, did you?' he remarked in good German as he started setting the fingers. 'Remarkable the number of people who have done that of late. I keep telling Sergeant Bull they shouldn't let the prisoners put such a high polish on it. But then, you know what you Krauts are when it comes to thoroughness.'

* * *

'So what happened when I told the Amis I wasn't going to sing?' he explained in a whisper to his comrade in the next cell. 'Someone pulled a shitty black hood over my head – I nearly creamed my drawers there and then – and they took me into another room. One of those Yids who do the interrogating said that there were several of my comrades hanging from the roof already. Of course, I said I didn't believe him, but you can never tell with the Ami bastards. Anyway, when I said I wasn't going to squeal on the Colonel, come what may, the Yid said: "I'm about to count to three. If you don't sing by then, you're going up!"

'I didn't know what the Yid meant, but I soon found out. They stuck a noose around my neck and hauled me up in the air. Great Crap on Christmas, I really thought that was it and I'd soon be looking at the potatoes from beneath! But just as everything started to go black, they let me down again. The Yid bastards did that to me *five shitty times*!' He gave a hoarse painful chuckle. 'But they didn't get me to betray the CO.'

* * *

As 1945 gave way to 1946, the survivors of SS Battle Group Wotan had still not broken, but von Dodenburg and the handful of officers among them knew they were rapidly reaching the end of their tether. Surprisingly enough, however, their Ami interrogators now turned their main attention to von Dodenburg himself.

On a cold January morning Bull came into his cell and ordered him to take his bedroll and shabby bits and pieces into another one further down the long grey echoing corridor. Surprisingly enough, the new cell was pleasantly warm. After the freezing cold of his old one, he relaxed and enjoyed the heat. The hours passed leadenly and the thick pipes running the length of the little cell grew hotter and hotter. Von Dodenburg started to grow uneasy. Why was he being honoured with so much heat?

Midday came, but not the usual thin gruel and hunk of stale bread. It seemed as if he had been forgotten altogether by the guards and the trustees from the Wehrmacht who served the food. But von Dodenburg was unconcerned about the food. The heat was becoming unbearable. He had ripped open his collar and taken off his threadbare grey jacket. Now he was sitting in his shirt-sleeves, black patches running down the back and great rings of black sweat-stained material under the armpits. Opaque pearls of sweat were beginning to gather at his eyebrows and hairline. His breath started to come in gasps. Wildly his eyes raced round the grey walls of the cell looking for some source of cold air.

Then he realized that they were softening him up for interrogation. Soon they would have him crying out frantically for release. He grasped the cell's only other piece of furniture beside the bed, a three-legged wooden stool. With all his strength he smashed it against the glass of the tiny window. But the glass did not give – it was reinforced with some kind of metal strips. Throwing a blanket over the red-hot steam pipes, he grabbed hold of them uppermost with both his hands. The stench of cloth burning was suffocating and the heat penetrated to his hands almost at once. But he only knew that he must get fresh air before he went wild screaming mad. Jamming his right foot against the wall to give himself leverage, he heaved with all his strength. Once, twice, three times. With a rending sound it came away from the wall and broke, filling the cell with hot clouds of steam. Choking and gulping, he grabbed his other blanket and rammed it into the hole. With the last of his strength, he used the pipe to launch a mighty blow against the little window. It shattered. Icy cold air came streaming in at once. He thrust his lathered, dripping face at the window, gulping in great breaths of the beautiful air, waiting as the heavy boots began to clatter down the long corridor.

* * *

They beat him for a solid week after that, coming for him regularly at the stroke of midnight, working him over in turns, slugging his body back and forth in the underground interrogation room. Twice they tried the bath treatment, grabbing his legs and thrusting his head deep into a bathful of icy water until he had almost blacked out and was gasping for air, before asking the same old question: 'All right, Kraut, are you gonna confess now that you ordered the goddam killings?'

Stubbornly von Dodenburg refused to give in. Somehow or other just as he was about to give in and let them have what they wanted to hear, he'd see Bull's vicious crimson face with its blood-shot, pig-like eyes and the hatred he had for his chief torturer would give him new strength; he would refuse to talk.

His interrogators were becoming desperate too. The trial had already been planned for March and still they had not obtained the confession they needed to convict the man the U.S. Press had been calling for months 'GI Enemy Number one'. Eisenhower's HQ in Frankfurt was screaming for results; the Department of the Army was already asking why the evidence the prosecution needed was not available. Had there been a hitch?

There had. The interrogators knew that all too well. The Krauts, demoralized and beaten as they were, were still sticking together. All the bribes, beatings and threats were having no effect on them or their commander; and twice Colonel Childers' guards had seized pencilled messages being passed from cell to cell, urging the Wotan men to 'remember, comrades, this is a battle like any other. We've beaten the Amis before and we'll do it again. Men of Wotan – standfast!'

Finally, in despair, the interrogators – with only three weeks to go to the trial – tried a new tack. On the morning of March 1st 1946, von Dodenburg was led out of his cell by Bull, taken to the wash-room and handed a razor-blade for his safety razor. 'Okay, Kraut,' the big NCO commanded, 'you've got exactly three minutes to shave and fancy yourself up. This morning we're gonna take you for a little ride in the country. Now make it snappy!'

It had snowed during the night and the stark winter countryside had been transformed. In its heavy white coat of snow it seemed tremendously beautiful to the shabby officer who had seen nothing but grey skies and greyer walls during the last few months. Von Dodenburg forgot the journey and Bull's hated heavy bulk next to him in the staff car, as they drove through the Bavarian back lanes to their mysterious destination.

An hour later the Ami car, followed by a half-track, filled with heavily armed guards, turned into the long drive leading up to an eighteenth-century Baroque mansion. Disinterested, von Dodenburg watched as the classical urns and ornamental stone stags, their slender backs covered in new snow, flashed by. What did it matter that the Amis were bringing him here? They could not hurt or humiliate him any more. Then they turned a corner and von Dodenburg shook himself out of his dreamy reverie at once. Round the sides of a big courtyard, that had once housed the mansion's stables, the survivors were standing in a double rank, shivering in the icy cold and stamping their frozen feet under the watchful eyes of a company of white-helmeted Ami snowdrops.

As the car braked to a halt, von Dodenburg flung a look at Bull and gasped: 'What's going on?'

Bull's reaction was a vicious dig in his ribs and a snarled command: 'Get out and move over into the centre of that goddam square!'

The SS men waited for what seemed an age, the only sound the chattering of their teeth and the persistent dry cough of a young trooper, who looked as if he might drop dead at any moment. Finally the door to the main building opened slowly and a plump, well-fed man stepped out, his body muffled in a dyed Ami greatcoat, one eye covered in a well-remembered black patch.

'Heaven, arse and twine,' someone gasped in the front rank of the panzer grenadiers, 'it's Sergeant Ochmann!'

But if Ochmann noticed the sudden excited reaction, he did not show it. Without even a single look at his former comrades, he walked confidentally to where Colonel Childers and Sergeant Bull were now standing and touched his head casually in salute, as if he were used to hob-nobbing with senior Ami officers every day of the week.

The door opened again. Two Amis in white overalls appeared, assisting a man in civilian clothes, who supported himself with difficulty on two white canes, the black and yellow spotted badge of the blind around his right arm, his eyes hidden behind thick dark spectacles. But it wasn't the man's blindness which caught the spectators' horrified attention; it was his face. Obviously he had been struck by a flame-thrower or something similar, for his face was a pink-puckered, frightening mess, with the eyebrows burnt away, the lips revealing naked horse teeth set in a terrifying permanent grin, and two holes where the ears had once been.

Slowly the human monster dragged itself closer to the centre of the square, tapping its frightening way through the snow with its canes until the two Amis finally halted it about ten paces from where a petrified von Dodenburg stood, a cold finger of fear tracing its icy way down the small of his back, the hair at the back of his head standing on end.

Colonel Childers seemed unaffected by the man's shocking

appearance. In a clear, completely controlled voice, he asked: 'Ex-Sergeant Ochmann, please tell us in German what was said by this man' – he indicated von Dodenburg – 'to the commander of the Panzer Grenadier Battalion on the afternoon of December 16th 1944.'

There was a sudden hush. The survivors hardly dare breathe, especially those who had taken part in the massacre. They craned forwards to hear their one-time NCO's reply.

Ochmann, his plump face red with good health, took his time. Obviously he was enjoying this moment for which the camp interrogators had been training him over the last seven days. 'As far as I can remember, sir,' he said at last, 'this officer told Major Harsch when the latter asked about the future of the prisoners we had just taken that he could – "take care of the prisoners".'

'What did he mean by that?' Childers snapped, his breath fogging in the icy air, despite the three whiskies he had consumed to warm himself up for this final attempt to break down the Wotan men and their stubborn bastard of a commander.

'Well, sir,' Ochmann replied. 'As I understood it, this officer meant Major Harsch should get rid of them.' He made a gesture of pulling back a rifle trigger. 'Kill them!'

'But that's not true!' von Dodenburg retorted hotly, forced to react at last. 'I simply meant he should solve the problem of what to do with the prisoners himself. I had other things on my mind at that moment. If Major Harsch were alive today, I'm sure he would confirm what I have just told you.'

Childers smiled thinly. 'But he is alive,' he said. 'Aren't you, Major?' He raised his voice and addressed the human monster, standing numbly between his two white-coated attendants. 'Major, can you hear me?'

As von Dodenburg stared in horrified silence at the man he had thought long dead on the bridge at Huy, the monster nodded his wreck of a head.

'Now then, Major Harsch, when Colonel von Dodenburg told you to take care of the prisoners what did he mean?'

The voice had a harsh, unnatural sound about it and seemed to come from far away, but there was no mistaking the word it uttered: they were simple, brutal and damning. 'Colonel von Dodenburg ordered me to kill the prisoners!'

Von Dodenburg opened his mouth to protest, but found he could not speak: his sense of outrage was too great. Childers nodded to the two attendants. Slowly they began to lead their patient back into the house. Childers turned his attention to the shocked survivors, their eyes round, wide and staring. 'Well, you heard what Major Harsch said,' he bellowed in his fluent if ungrammatical German. 'Why should you take the can back for something you were ordered to do? A CO is responsible for the actions of his men, especially when he is as experienced as yours was, and so many of you were virtually new recruits to the Army. Let him pay the penalty – not you.' He paused and licked his fat lips. He knew this was the moment of truth. At the price of his own freedom Ochmann had already revealed to the interrogators those among the survivors who had participated in the massacre. In view of the fact that those men now knew Ochmann and Harsch were still alive, they might be prepared to save their own skins by denouncing their CO. 'Well, you heard me! Some of you have committed crimes. But you did so under orders. We Americans are not after you little fish. If you'll play ball with us, we'll play ball with you.' His whisky-thick voice rose to a crescendo. 'Now come on – *who heard Colonel von Dodenburg order Major Harsch to kill the American prisoner*?'

'I did!' an impassioned voice screamed. '*I did!*' It was the blond trooper who had fired the first shot, tears of self-pity streaming down his face. 'I don't want to die for something I didn't do!' He sank on his knees in the snow, writhing from side to side.

'I did as well,' another voice joined in. 'He said it! I was standing close by! I heard him say it too!' The bareheaded corporal, who had gone through the bloody ranks of the Americans after the shooting, kicking them to check if they were dead and laughing as he had finished those off who weren't, suddenly started to scream invective at the officer.

Now the accusations and obscenities started to flood in from all sides, as if the blind Major's appearance had broken a long established dam of silence and secrecy. '*Traitor . . . gangster . . . murderer*' – the cries, shrill, fervent and hysterical, filled the air, while von Dodenburg's lack-lustre eyes filled with horror at the final breakdown of loyalty, his one good hand raised as if he could ward them off physically. Suddenly one of the men in the front rank hawked and spat at him. It was the blond giant who had once boasted he would march down the *Unter den Linden* with him. Von Dodenburg retched with shock. Another bent and scooped up a fistful of snow. Before the guards could stop him, he had flung it with all his strength at his former CO. Von Dodenburg staggered as it caught him on the chin. They started pelting him on all sides, while Childers laughed. Suddenly von Dodenburg could stand it no longer.

Before anyone could stop him, he had turned and begun to run awkwardly, his leg hurting like hell, his head ducked into his shoulders, back muscles tensed for the smash of the bullets which must come and end his miserable existence.

But they didn't come. Angry surprised cries followed him. That was all. He slowed down, making himself an easier target. Still there was no order to fire. He stopped altogether and supported himself weakly against a tree, his chest heaving with the strain of the sudden violent exertion.

The next instant, Bull's shaven head rammed home into his guts. He screamed with pain and went down, Bull's massive weight crushing him. A hard fist crashed into his face. Blood spurted from his nose. The fist smashed down again. Bull grunted pleasurably and hit him once more. Through the red shivering mist, Colonel Childers's fat, pleased face loomed up and his beady blue eyes stared down at the bleeding German officer with unconcealed delight.

'No, my dear Colonel von Dodenburg,' he said softly, 'you're not going to get away with it as easy as that. A bullet is too good for you. No, you'll stand your trial and die at the end of a rope like the rotten criminal trash you are.'

Then the voice faded to nothing as von Dodenburg's bloody head slipped to one side, as he fell into the blessed state of unconsciousness.

2

The prosecutor, a lean, dried-up lawyer from the Mid-West, who affected gold-rimmed pince-nez, opened his case with an aggressive attack on the prisoner. He knew that if he won this case, he would be promoted to colonel – the senior judge advocate in Frankfurt had promised him the promotion on his word of honour – and the future job of prosecuting the senior SS generals in U.S. hands, such Dietrich and Kraemer. Not that he was concerned much about them, but the publicity he'd get stateside on the von Dodenburg trial and his retirement rank of colonel when he quit the service in ten month's time wouldn't do his civilian practice any harm.

'We all know,' he said, 'what Adolf Hitler's order to his SS generals was in December 1944. They were to cause as much terror as possible and break enemy resistance with every means at their disposal. This criminal here,' he pointed a finger at a completely unmoved von Dodenburg, 'who had already shown what a barbarian he was in Russia and Italy, was just the man to carry that order out. Ambitious, one hundred and ten per cent fanatical Nazi, Kuno von Dodenburg, he – of all the SS criminals – would stop at nothing in his attempts to please his beloved Führer.' He raised his voice melodramtically, 'Your honour, I ask this court to waste no time on that beast in human clothing sitting in the dock. There is only one possible sentence that can be passed on such a monster – *death*!'

In the dock, Kuno von Dodenburg took out his handkerchief and blew his nose. The prosecutor glared at him. But such minor harassment did not put him off his stride. Rapidly he built up his case against the accused. Ochmann and Harsch were summoned as witnesses. 'Men, whose broken bodies testify that they have suffered enough and have paid for the errors of their ways – men who now want to pay their debt to society' – and gave their damning testimony.

They were followed by a series of young troopers whose spirit had been broken by the months of torture in the interrogation camp or who were now eager to save their own skins, fearful of what the prosecution's two chief witnesses knew about them. 'Cogs in a machine of death, all of them,' as the prosecutor explained, 'dripping with blood instead of oil. One day they, too, will have to answer to the court for their crimes. But their crimes pale into insignificance beside those of that monster in the dock there who ordered them to commit their crimes.'

And so it went on, hour after hour, day after day. Von Dodenburg's sweating, scared civilian advocate in his black gown was no match for the American and the sheer weight of his evidence. When the now Master-Sergeant Abraham Rosenbloom, his chest ablaze with decorations and the blue enamel combat infantryman's badge, was produced to give his damning evidence, ending it with the dramatic accusation: '*He* was the man who gave the order to kill those boys in cold blood,' the German lawyer gave up completely.

Twice von Dodenburg tried to convince him that most of the prosecution's witnesses' statements had been gained under duress, but the lawyer's sole reply was to shake his head and whisper fearfully: 'But I couldn't say the Amis tortured their prisoners, could I? How long do you think I'd be in business in the U.S. Zone of Occupation if I did?' In the end von Dodenburg gave up and let things take their course, staring out of the window most of the time in plain boredom. He'd had it. Why bother? Thus he never noticed the big, blowsy woman, among the handful of civilians allowed into the trial for publicity purposes, who watched him the whole while in anxious concern.

* * *

Colonel Kuno von Dodenburg was sentenced on the morning of April 10th 1946. Just before ten o'clock that morning, he was led into the little court by an immaculate Bull and two other guards and halted in front of the panel of seven judges, all in their Class A uniforms. General Dalby, the president of the court, a ramrod-stiff infantryman, who had been wounded in the Battle of the Bulge, looked at the German prisoner in obvious distaste, then fumbled with steel-rimmed GI spectacles before he began to read the details of the court's findings.

Von Dodenburg found his mind wandering. Outside the spring sunshine was warming the grey courtyard and he remembered that it had been on such a day when the Wotan had first paraded for Adolf Hitler, a month before their baptism of fire in Belgium. How proud, how young, how confident he had felt then! Now he was worn and old, and just as he had betrayed those confident young men time and time again over these last five years, sending them to their deaths on impossible missions, they had betrayed him in the end. The great dream which had sent them marching all over Europe in one mighty conquest after another was over; there was nothing left for him now but to die.

At the dais, General Dalby cleared his throat before he read the last sentence on the paper held in his hands, that were now beginning to tremble a little with tension. 'The court sentences you – to death by hanging!'

There was an instant's silence. Suddenly everyone was staring at the thin man in the shabby field-grey uniform, devoid of any badge of rank, his crippled arm hanging limpy down his side. Von Dodenburg pursed his lips. Then the words came – in English, audible right to the final row of the court! 'Thank you, sir.'

Von Dodenburg turned smartly to the right, with just a trace of that old time Wotan military precision, and marched back the way he had come. Behind him in the hushed court, the big blowsy woman started to sob softly.

* * *

Two days later von Dodenburg, dressed in the red jacket of the condemned, had a visitor. He was lying apathetically on his bunk, hands behind his head, staring at the peeling ceiling when Bull opened the door and bellowed: 'Okay, Kraut, on ya feet. The CO's allowed you a visitor. Your old lady's here.'

Von Dodenburg sat up. 'What did you say?' he exclaimed.

Bull stared down at him, his piglike little eyes full of contempt for the German whom they had finally broken. 'What's the matter with you, Kraut? Got wax in ya ears or something! I said your mother's here to see ya.'

'*Mother—*' Von Dodenburg caught himself just in time. His mother had been dead these ten years. 'Oh, all right, Sergeant.' Slowly, trying to hide the sudden nervous twitching of his left cheek, he rose to his feet and followed Bull into the grey echoing corridor.

'Mother' was a big woman of about forty, dressed in a black skirt that was much too short for her massive flanks and a white silk blouse under which her massive breasts shivered every time she breathed. She took the handkerchief she had pressed to her nose away as soon as he entered, followed by Bull's massive figure.

'All right,' Bull said, 'ya've got exactly ten minutes, thanks to the CO's soft heart.' He planted himself on the chair in the far corner of the room in obvious boredom. 'And no touching each other or passing anything over. OK you silly old cow,' with a nod of his big cropped head, he indicated the two chairs facing each other, 'Park ya fat keester on that!'

Hurriedly the two of them sat down. 'How good it is to see you again, my son,' the woman quavered, her breasts trembling under the shimmering silk.

Von Dodenburg's heart missed a beat. The strange woman's accent was pure Ardennes German!

'Who are you, in three devils' name?' he hissed.

The fat woman pulled a severe warning face. It said 'calm down – don't give me away'. 'A good friend of yours sent me, sir,' she said slowly and softly. 'He wants to help you.'

'Who?'

'He told me not to tell you,' she replied, anxiously peeping out of the corner of her eye at Bull's massive frame sprawled out in the corner, an old copy of *Yank* magazine held in his big bruiser's hands. 'These terrible days, you can never be too sure. You understand, sir?'

Von Dodenburg nodded, a sudden hope surging within him.

'But you must not show any surprise when he comes to see you. He told me that to emphasize that. You must not show any surprise. Please promise that!'

'Yes, yes, I promise,' he swore eagerly. 'But how is he – whoever the hell he is – going to get into here?'

The fat woman's tense look vanished for the first time. She laughed softly, 'You know him – nothing can stop him. He's coming in as your father . . .'

* * *

But the days passed and no suddenly resurrected father appeared. Every morning von Dodenburg was awake at six, listening to the spring chatter of the birds outside, impatiently waiting for Bull to call him to receive his visitor; and every morning he was disappointed, spending the rest of the day mooning about, hardly touching his food so that Bull, a malicious grin on his big red face, would comment: 'What's up, Kraut? Starting to get nervous? It's only three weeks now, isn't it, before they string you up!'

Nights were hell. He would toss and turn on his narrow bunk, listening to the sighs and groans of the other prisoners, his fevered brain racing. Who might his mysterious visitor be? Could he have some connection with the legendary 'Spider Organization', which according to the prison grapevine, was an SS outfit that conveyed wanted men to safety? Were they going to try to get him out and run him along the BB-line[1] to Austria and from thence into Italy with its many ports, leading to South America? So many questions – with so few answers.

A week passed. Still no visitor. He began to despair. Time was running out. In ten days that macabre little procession of guards, Chaplain and hangman would be coming to fetch him to end his life in the dark womb of the underground room. He began to wonder whether his imagination was not playing him tricks; perhaps he had never received that strange female visitor after all!

Then on a rainy April morning when he had given up hope, Bull opened the door of his cell and jerked his big thumb at the

[1] A reputed Nazi escape route – the Bremen-Bari Line. (*Transl.*)

unhappy prisoner. 'Okay, Kraut. Visitor. Move it! Your old man's here!'

His 'father' was standing opposite the big barred window, his massive shoulders threatening to burst the tight shiny fabric of his black civilian suit as he stared out pensively at the dripping rain.

'Your son,' Bull announced and dropped gloomily into his usual chair. 'Ya've got ten minutes. No more – no less. Kay?'

The man in the black suit nodded, but did not turn round; it was as if he were waiting until the Ami NCO had buried his big crimson face in his cheap book. Slowly he turned, a bunch of drooping violets clasped ludicrously in his fist.

Von Dodenburg bit his lip hard to prevent the cry of recognition escaping from his throat! 'Father' winked and raised his right leg slightly, as if he were going to give one of his celebrated musical farts of so long ago. Von Dodenburg's eyes filled with sudden tears. Slowly 'Father' limped towards him and thrust the drooping violets into his good hand. 'There you are, my poor dear boy,' he said in that well-known waterfront voice for Bull's benefit just in case he were watching them. 'A handful of flowers to remind you of the spring.' His pious look vanished for an instant and out of the corner of his big mouth he hissed. 'For Chrissake, don't throw the wrapping paper away, sir.'

'By the great whore of Buxtehude,' von Dodenburg hissed happily, 'How good it is to see you again, Schulze!'

The big ex-docker pulled a face. 'Never use that name, sir!' he warned. 'I'm Emile Fagnoul now, sir, a shitty Belgie civilian, companion of the great Ardennes mare who came to visit you the other day and the owner of one of the nicest little knocking shops in Dachau you've ever seen. Every taste catered for. Special demonstrations for our rich American Allies.' He sighed sadly. 'How poor old Matzie would have liked it! It was always the poor little cripple's dream to be able to retire to a whorehouse.'

'But how the devil—'

Schulze held up his hand to stop the burst of questions. 'No time for that now, sir. We've only got a few minutes more.

Suffice to say that if it hadn't been for that great Ardennes mare when you hid me in that forest last year, I'd be looking at the potatoes from below now. She saved my turnip, she did.' He shook his head in fond memory. 'Great crap on the Christmas Tree, doesn't she have plenty of meat in that blouse of hers! Wow sir, get this. I'm gonna get you out of this place sharpish. But you've got to get yourself transferred to the dock first of all. The bone-menders are not so strong on security. That's one. Two,' he ticked it off on his big fingers, 'there's a sewer leading from the hospital. Full of crap – up to here. But you've been through worse during the war, sir. You'll just have to grin and bear it. Once you're though that – the details are on the wrapping paper – you're in the camp courtyard and—'

'But Schulze,' interrupted von Dodenburg. 'There's the courtyard wall. It's at least ten metres high and I couldn't scale it with this rotten flipper of mine.' He looked down angrily at his paralysed hand.

'Don't you worry your head about that sir. Schulze'll take care of that little problem.'

'How do you mean?'

'Easy, sir, I'm coming in to meet you on Tuesday night. Remember that – *Tuesday night*!'

In the corner, Bull was rising slowly to his feet. His little eyes fell on the flowers. 'What the hell have you got there, Kraut?' he asked suspiciously.

Schulze beat von Dodenburg to it. In his newly acquired English, he said: 'It is the last time I am seeing my son, Captain. I am thinking he is liking some sweet flowers.'

Bull looked at him and then at his ashen-faced 'son'; then he shrugged carelessly. 'Okay, I'll see to it personally that they're put on his grave next week.' He sniggered unpleasantly. 'Kay, Pop, now beat it, will ya . . .'

3

Monday. The guard went slowly down the waiting line of prisoners, stripped to the waist and poised in front of the greasy, scummed, zinc wash-basins of the abolutions, handing a razor blade to each man, counting them off silently to himself. Beyond them another line of men squatted on the latrines, straining in the doorless cubicles, knowing that they had exactly three minutes to complete the business before it was their turn to step forwards – at the guard's command – to enjoy the luxury of the weekly shave.

The big red-haired PFC finished. 'Kay, you guys, everybody got a blade? You've got exactly three minutes from *now.*'

They ducked their bearded faces at once in handfuls of icy water, trying to soften up the beard the best they could. One or two of them had slivers of preciously hoarded soap, but most of them, including von Dodenburg, had to make do with the icy water. On this particular Monday, von Dodenburg was not worried about the closeness of his shave. Hastily he scraped the blunt blade the length of his cheek, wincing with pain, as it tore at his skin. He didn't care. The main thing was that the Ami guard saw he was cleanly shaven when he came to collect his blade. He nicked his chin. But he had no time to stop the bleeding. His eyes were too busy searching for a likely candidate among the young men all around him. Then he spotted him. The blond giant who had testified against him during the trial. He was only two sinks away, busy scrubbing his cheeks with a sliver of soap, visibly enjoying the simple pleasure.

'One more minute, you guys,' snapped the guard from where he leaned against the wall.

Von Dodenburg swiftly dried his face and taking out the blade, placed it on the dripping shelf in front of him so the guard could pick it up. Von Dodenburg took out the salt and sprinkled it on his toothbrush. He commenced brushing his teeth with a great show of determination. Now the men from the latrines were beginning to line up, ready for their shave. Across the way the blond giant had taken out his blade and placed it on the ledge. Von Dodenburg quickly bent his head under the running tap and took in a mouthful of the icy water. He pushed his neighbour and without a moment's hesitation sprayed it directly into the surprised boy's face.

'Say, what the hell are you trying to do?' he spluttered angrily, blinded for a moment.

'You know what I think of you,' von Dodenburg answered coldly. 'You're a traitor—'

'*Traitor*,' roared the boy and leaning forwards, launched a powerful right at his former CO. 'I'll show you who's a traitor!'

Hastily the men nearest scattered. Von Dodenburg ducked easily, dropping the blade into his cuff. A bowl overturned. Dirty water streamed everywhere. 'You heard, what I said!' he yelled. 'You betrayed me—'

'All right, knock it off!' yelled the suddenly alarmed guard. 'That's enough of that, you Krauts!' His big hand dropped significantly to the holster of his 45.

The big blond, the water still dripping from his offended-looking face, let his fists fall sullenly. Von Dodenburg smiled to himself and stepped back to his place, as the guard started coming down the line collecting the blades, silently counting them off as the prisoners dropped them into the box.

He passed von Dodenburg, flashed him a suspicious look, collected his blade and continued his slow progress. At the latrines the other group were beginning to strip off their shirts. Suddenly the guard stopped in front of the big blond trooper.

'Where's the blade,' he demanded, 'Everybody's gotta turn in a blade!'

The blond looked at him in bewilderment. 'But it was there,' he indicated the shelf.

'Sure, and if my aunt Fanny had a moustache, she'd be my uncle Joe,' the guard said cynically. 'Check on the floor to see if you've dropped it, you big dumb Kraut.'

The blond trooper dropped to his knees and began searching the damp trough beneath the sinks for the blade, while the guard watched him suspiciously. A moment later he rose shaking his head in bewilderment. 'It isn't there. I know I put it on the shelf.'

'Yeah,' the guard said impatiently. 'But everybody's gotta turn in a blade, buddy. Without it, you don't leave this craphouse – *ever*.'

'But, I tell you, I had it,' the trooper protested. 'I put it—'

The guard drew his pistol. 'Okay, all you guys who just shaved – over against that wall. Move it now!' He waved the 45 threateningly. As they shuffled towards the wall, his suspicious gaze not letting them out of sight for one moment, the guard tugged out his whistle and blew three sharp blasts on it.

Seconds later the washhouse was filled with excited Amis, while the angry guard related his story. It was the chance for which von Dodenburg had been waiting. Swiftly, feeling for the blade beneath the material of his cuff, he broke it in two and palmed one half.

'Okay,' the guard snapped. 'All you guys drop your slacks – quick! Then up against the wall, with yer legs spread and your arms outstretched! Come on now – make it goddam snappy!'

The guards began to pass among them, running their hands down their bodies, peering between their legs in case they had attempted to hide the blade in their body hair. Von Dodenburg, who had jostled himself into positon next to the blond, tensed. He caught his breath. It was now or never. A guard started to run his hands down the blond's big body, as another approached him. Praying as he had never prayed these last ten years or more, he dropped the half a blade on the floor at the blond's feet.

The guard spotted it at once. 'Here it is Joe!' he yelled. The one coming to search von Dodenburg stopped in his tracks. 'The bastard must have stuck it in his mouth – there's blood on it – and broke it up!'

The red-haired PFC, flushed with anger, rammed the muzzle of his 45 viciously into the blond's back. The trooper groaned and staggered. 'So it was you after all!' he cried.

'Giving me all that goddam chicken shit about not having it! Well, Charlie Erzenberger is not the kinda guy to take that kind of sass.' He rammed the gun home again with all his strength. The blond went down on his knees, his face pale, his mouth open with pain. 'Brother, when I'm finished with you back in the cells, you'll goddam wish you'd have committed suicide straight away.' His mouth curled into a cruel smile. 'Kraut, it's gonna give me the greatest of pleasure to nail your goddam Heinie hide to the barn! Okay, the rest of you guys – let's move it outa here!'

Fighting to control his smile of triumph with the bloody other half of the broken razor blade clenched in his good hand, von Dodenburg allowed himself to be hustled outside. Operation Rescue was under way.

*　　*　　*

Von Dodenburg waited until the Judas Hole had been slid back into position and the soft-soled tread of the night guard had started to pass up the sleeping corridor. Now all was silent again, save for the snores of some happy prisoner able to forget the misery of the camp for a few hours. He checked the cell in the thin yellow light of the bulb in the ceiling protected from damage by its barbed-wire casing. Everything all right. Swiftly he pulled the blade from its hiding place and tested its sharpness with his thumb. It wasn't too good, but it would serve its purpose.

He flashed a last look at the Judas Hole. No suspicious Ami eye peered in at him. Carefully he pulled the blankets over his head, as prescribed by camp orders, leaving the required amount of his face visible so that any night guard who cared could check up that the condemned man would not escape the gallows by suicide or the happy oblivion of dying in his sleep.

With his good hand, he fumbled for the wrist of his left hand under the blankets and found it. He ran his thumb across the wrist for the artery he sought. Taking a deep breath, he drew the blade deliberately across the wrist, sawing at the vein. He winced and bit back the yelp of pain just in time. He peered down for an instant. Nothing! Then slowly a thin red line began to appear across the pale length of his wrist. His 'suicide' attempt was going according to plan.

The flow of blood started to thicken. He gritted his teeth and sliced his wrist again – and again. The blood began to pour out of the multiple wounds. The pain was almost unbearable. With his good hand, he stuffed the top of the blanket into his mouth and hacked at the wrist one more time. Then he let the blade drop from his nerveless fingers, his moans stiffled by the blanket, and waited.

An hour passed. His head was beginning to buzz. A mist hovered in front of his eyes. Beneath the blankets everything was wet and sticky with blood. He felt himself getting weaker by the minute. Still he hung on. He had to look so bad that they would take him to the hospital.

At two o'clock he knew he couldn't wait any longer, otherwise he would bleed to death. As the prison clock finished striking the hour, he pushed back the blankets weakly. The bed was full of thick blood. Groggily he rose to his feet. His legs felt as if they were made of jelly. Twice he collapsed and only raised himself by a sheer effort of will, as he staggered to the door. With all his remaining strength he banged his tin jug against the thick wood and cried '*Guard – help me . . . I'm . . .!*'

Seconds later the door crashed open. The guard gasped with horror and bellowed a plea for assistance. Just before he blacked out completely, von Dodenburg heard an enraged Bull yell: 'Get that goddam Kraut bastard to the hospital before he croaks on me!' His boot crashed into von Dodenburg's side. 'He's not gonna escape the necktie party I've got planned for the bugger.'

In spite of the pain, von Dodenburg grinned. He had done it.

* * *

It was raining hard, coming down out of the night sky in straight sheets, broken only by the violet flashes of lightning which had followed the thunder. Up in the little wooden tower, the red-haired PFC buried his head even deeper into the collar of his slicker, the rain pouring off his helmet-liner and down the back of his neck unpleasantly. Again he cursed the Kraut who had built the tower, for not having provided it with a roof; the head shirt for having put him on the guard roster for such a night; and the prisoners, who were his reason for being outside at one o'clock in the morning instead of in bed with one of the plump little whores at Emile's cathouse.

A vivid flash of lightning close by made him start suddenly. He huddled deeper into his rubber slicker and shivered with the cold wetness of it. Somewhere a clock struck the quarter. Another ninety minutes and he'd be relieved. Then he'd be able to get at the bottle of German potato schnapps he had stashed away in the guard-room. Ninety more minutes! Slinging his M-I, its muzzle protected from the rain by a condom, more securely over his shoulder, he began to walk the square of the watch tower, eyes narrowed against the driving rain.

The clock in the town below struck the half hour. The red-haired PFC opened his eyes. In the same instant, there was a great echoing clap of thunder. Lightning zig-zagged fierily across the night sky. He closed his eyes, momentarily blinded, but not before he had caught a glimpse of somebody crouching dark and menacing at the base of the watch-tower.

'What should he do?' the question flashed through his mind as he opened his eyes to peer into the pitch-blackness below. Should he call the head shirt? Bull would have the nuts off him, if there were nothing down there after all. He bit his lip, the pouring rain and wet misery forgotten now, as he tried to penetrate the thick gloom in search of the mysterious figure.

Protectively he dropped on one knee. Whipping off the condom, he rested his M-I on the railing. He jerked the bolt back and clicked the safety off. If there were anybody down there in the compound, he was going to get his head blasted off the minute he showed himself – and no goddam messing. 'Okay, buddy,' he snarled between gritted teeth, 'let's be goddam having you!'

Again lightning stabbed the sky. Almost instinctively, the red-haired PFC jerked the trigger of his rifle. The sound of the single shot was drowned by the greater noise. His scream of pain ended in a thick muffled grunt, as the terrible blow crashed into the base of his neck and he went down, reeling sickeningly into the blackness.

* * *

Cautiously von Dodenburg flicked open his eyes. The soft-shoed orderly had departed, leaving them apparently sleeping in the white-painted severe hospital room, its sole decoration the two steel cots and the two bedside tables, complete with the drugs for the morning which the medical orderly had just deposited there.

He looked over at the room's other occupant – the one-armed youth who was going to be brought to trial in a week's time, and who had tried to commit suicide by swallowing the disinfectant he had stolen from the Ami officers' latrines. He was snoring hoarsely through his nose, his mouth filled with the gadgets the Amis had placed there in an attempt to save his ruined throat. The Americans had kept him under heavy sedation ever since he had been delivered into the hospital two hours after himself.

Von Dodenburg raised himself weakly from the bed and placed his legs gingerly on the floor. They felt like rubber. Cautiously he raised himself using his good hand and nearly fell over. He shook his head to clear the black fog which had threatened to overcome him. He knew from the wrapping paper instructions that now he had exactly sixty minutes to find the sewer, scramble through it and get into the courtyard where – God willing– Schulze would be waiting for him. He must get to his feet and get on with it! The alternative was death at the end of an Ami rope. Gritting his teeth, feeling the blood pounding madly in his temples, he started to raise himself. Slowly and painfully, still clad in the prison nightshirt, his only clothing, he began to pad down the long, dark corridor.

Somewhere to his right, he heard low voices and the soft hum of a radio tuned in to an American station. The orderlies' room! He could see the yellow light seeping through the bottom of the door. 'Jones is now first base . . . Yeah, folks, this one really looks as if it's gonna be a triple hitter . . .' the commentator's excited voice went on and on; and von Dodenburg was eternally grateful to the unknown American, for it covered the painfully slow shuffle of his bare feet, as he worked his way past the door and on along the corridor, which seemed to stretch for kilometres ahead of him.

Once he staggered violently and had to support himself against the wall to prevent himself fainting in his tracks. Once, too, a sudden sharp noise startled him violently and set his heart off, beating like a trip-hammer. But it was only the thick cough of some unfortunate youth dying of TB, as so many of the former Wotan men were now, after a winter of prison cells and short rations.

At last he made it. Bending painfully, he started to use the broompole he had found in the latrine to lever up the lid. It refused to give. He renewed his efforts. Time was ticking away. With the sweat standing on his forehead in great beads, he finally managed to push it open. The stench was overpowering. He gagged throatily and prevented himself from retching just in time. He dropped the pole and stared down at the steaming, foetid mass that lined the bottom of the downward-sloping tunnel into which streams of – what he hoped was – muddy water trickled continually. Swiftly he lifted up his long nightshirt and ripped off its base. With his good hand, he wrapped the piece of material around his mouth, and sat down at the edge of the open sewer. There was no sound save for that of the trickle of water below and the drip-drip of some leaky tap into a zinc basin somewhere behind him. Taking a deep breath, he dropped feet-first into the mire. He was on his way!

* * *

Master Sergeant Ed Bull was in a bad mood. His night with the Kraut whore he had picked up in his favourite downtown bar had not ended the way he had intended. They had danced a while, going through the hectic motions of what the young Kraut dames called a 'trembling fox', and he had plied the buxom blonde with plenty of cheap Kraut black-market champagne. 'Hell,' he had boasted to her, flinging another pack of *Luckies* on the table to buy a further bottle, 'for a carton of 'em, I could have the goddam salesman, baby!' But then when he had gotten her to her little flat in one of the town centre's bombed-out villas, everything seemed to go wrong.

The little Kraut whore – drunk and giggling – had stripped completely naked. In the dusky-red light on the bed, she had lain back, holding up her heavy breasts to him invitingly, her taut thighs spread to display the wet V of hair, and in a strained, excited voice had urged him to come in to her. He had stripped hurriedly, tearing off his shoes to stand in front of her in all his heavy animal nakedness. It was then he had found out it wouldn't work.

At first she had not noticed. She had thought he was teasing her to new heights of ecstasy. She had squeezed her breasts and wriggled her nubile little body seductively, lying spread-eagled and expectant. 'Come on – quick,' she had breathed passionately. 'I want you. Now!'

'I can't,' he had stammered, his big round face suddenly crimson. 'It won't . . . won't work.'

For what had seemed an age, she had looked up at him in blank amzement; then she had flung back her head and begun to laugh, the tears streaming down her drunken young face. 'Can't . . . can't do . . . it,' she had pointed a finger at his big, naked useless body and gone off again into a paroxysm of laughter.

Suddenly a great burning rage had overcome him. His fist had slammed into her mocking bitch's face. Her laughter had ended in a smothered scream of pain, as her nose burst and the thick red blood had begun to stream down her face. A second later he had started to beat the hell out of her with his fists. But even when she had become a whimpering bloody wreck on the bed, trying to stem the flow of blood with her black lace panties, he had not overcome that blow to his male pride and sexual prowess.

Now as he plodded morosely back to the prison, the heavy rain beating on his brutal shoulders, his mood as black as the night, he could simply not forget her contemptuous laughter and those choked words, which she had flung after him: 'You should be like Washington – my black boyfriend – now he can do it all the time . . . Boy, has he got a big one! And does he know how to use it . . .'

He passed through the gate, snapping at the guard who asked him for his ID card that he'd better hold his trap if he didn't want a knuckle sandwich in it; the head shirt didn't show his 'goddam crappy ID to no one!' Hardly noticing the rain which was soaking through his white trench coat, he stamped heavily towards his quarters, his mind full of the whore's laughter, the rage still burning within him. Then all of a sudden he stopped. A strange sort of scratching noise was coming from the sewer manhole cover, a matter of twenty yards away. Bull's rage vanished. He pulled out the looted Walther Police Special, which he always carried with him off duty – you could never trust the Krauts – and crouched there expectantly.

For a couple of moments nothing happened, as if who – or whatever – had been scratching down there in the sewer had heard his heavy footsteps. Then slowly the sewer lid started to rise. Bull tensed, finger gripping the trigger alertly, as the rain continued to pour down. The night air was filled with the stench of the sewer. The waiting American realized that it could only contain an escaping prisoner. An evil grin began to spread across his big, red, rain-lashed face. Brother, the Kraut was really going to be in for a surprise! The way he felt at the moment, he'd nail the bastard's skin to the barn – and then some! He started to feel a warm glow of anticipation.

The lid toppled to the ground with a faint metallic clatter. A dark head appeared above the surface of the cobbled courtyard. Infinitely slowly, as if the escapee was at the end of his strength, the prisoner started to lever himself out of the stinking hole. Bull narrowed his eyes and tried to penetrate the driving rain, but he couldn't make out the man's features, even though he knew that the man *must* be an escaping prisoner.

He held his breath. The man was coming towards him. Suddenly the lightning sliced the darkness. But it was sufficient for Bull to recognize the skinny German escapee. It was that Kraut Colonel – von Dodenburg! He prevented himself from laughing aloud only just in time. This, he was going to enjoy. Dropping his pistol back into the pocket of his trenchcoat, he breathed on the knuckles of his right hand and straightened up.

'Going for a little hike, Kraut?' he asked softly.

Von Dodenburg started violently. 'Who's there?'

'Who the goddam hell, do you think,' that hated voice replied menacingly, '*Santa Claus?*'

Von Dodenburg's throat tightened. For a moment he seemed paralysed, unable to move, the rain streaming down and soaking his night shirt, sudden puddles forming at his naked feet. Then he ducked, and charged.

Bull was too quick for him. He caught the German officer easily in his big hands. 'Ner, it's not gonna be that easy to catch old Bull off guard, Kraut,' he grunted, his sausagelike fingers wrenching at von Dodenburg's hair. Von Dodenburg screamed and tried to wriggle free, despair lending strength to his weakened body. Bull held on without even having to breathe hard. 'Go on, Kraut, have fun – it's the last you're gonna have this side of the grave.' Holding on to the wildly struggling man with a big hand, he pulled back his right fist ready to smash it into von Dodenburg's face.

But suddenly a massive shape detached itself from the streaming gloom and smashed into Bull's back. He groaned and let go of von Dodenburg. Staggering forward he crashed into the wall. Schulze was on him in a flash. He smashed his fist into Bull's face. The Ami's nose-bone smashed like dry twigs and the blood spurted out of his nose in red gobs, but still Bull didn't go down. He shook his head, grabbed Schulze's wrist and twisted round, thrusting his hip in to the other man's stomach. Schulze swallowed a scream as he flew through the air and landed on his back with all the wind knocked out of him. Bull dived forward. In the last instant, Schulze, gasping for breath, rolled to one side. Bull landed on the soaked cobbles purposelessly.

With surprising agility for he was on his feet again in an instant, wiping the blood from his face with a mud-stained paw. 'All right, you Kraut zombie, come and get me!' he breathed, circling the other man, crouched on the ground on one knee, his big hands extended.

Schulze hesitated. He knew he had met his match. In the old days on the waterfront, he had had his share of brawls, with sailors from all nations. But this one was no dummy; he would fight as dirty as any seaman Schulze had ever known. It wouldn't do to play with him. Slowly he began to rise to his feet. The two men eyed each other through the streaming rain, hands formed to claws, waiting for the advantage they needed. Suddenly Schulze saw his. The Ami had his foot poised just above the open sewer. One step backwards and he would be caught off guard.

Bull moved. In the same moment, Schulze dived forward. They collided with a sickening thud. As Bull stumbled into the hole with one foot, Schulze rammed his elbow into the Ami's face. Bull screamed and went down on one knee, fighting desperately to keep his balance.

'Now, you Ami currant-crapper!' Schulze roared triumphantly and raised his big booted foot to ram it into the fallen man's face. 'You better say your shitty—'

Schulze screamed as Bull reached up, grabbed his exposed genitals and twisted them cruelly to the right. Tearing himself away, he went down, head huddled to his stomach, his mouth full of sudden vomit, little choked noises of pain escaping through his gritted teeth.

Bull rose slowly, towering over the man writhing back and forth on the cobbles, hands clasped to his genitals, trying to soothe the terrible agony. With infinite pleasure, he raised his right foot over the white blur of the unknown German's face. 'Okay Kraut,' he breathed softly, his mind full of the whore's last terrible words to him, 'now try this one on for size.' He grunted and started to crash the big cruel boot down on Schulze's face.

With the last of his strength, von Dodenburg brought the sewer lid down on the back of Bull's head. He crashed to his knees, blood spurting from his smashed skull. Von Dodenburg hit him again, feeling the weight of the lid tearing his bones from their sockets. Still Bull did not fall. Meaningless animal noises were escaping from his lips, but the big Ami NCO was not yet dead. 'Christ on a crutch, man!' cursed von Dodenburg, his face contorted with hate, '*will you never die!*' He hit him one last time. Bull's scream of agony died under the impact of that final blow. As he smacked to the wet cobbles something snapped and Master Sergeant Ed Bull was dead at last.

* * *

'Heaven, arse and twine, do you pong, sir!' Schulze said shakily. 'Worse than poor old Matzie after he'd had some of that pea soup from the kitchen bulls in the old days!'

'I was down that damn sewer, Schulze,' von Dodenburg answered weakly, squatting in the rain next to Bull's dead body. 'What do you expect?'

'These things are sent to try us, sir.'

'Well, try me too,' von Dodenburg answered, feeling the strength ebbing out of him every second. 'I'm ... absolutely beat ...'

Schulze laughed drily. 'Not to worry, sir. You know Wotan's old motto – march or croak! And I'm not about to croak at this particular moment.' Putting one big foot on Bull's dead chest to brace himself, he put his arm around von Dodenburg and lifted him as easily as if he were a child. 'Come on, Colonel, I think you've been a guest of our American friends long enough ...'

4

Slowly but steadily, the two men tramped down the dusty white Bavarian farm road, advancing towards the gleaming mountain peak which marked the frontier with Austria. On this hot June day there was little left to reveal that there had once been a war fought here and that young men had died suddenly and violently in these peaceful fields: a rusting Sherman, its tracks gone; an 88 mm, its shattered muzzle pointing up a lane waiting for an enemy who would never come now; a bullet-pocked wall; a cluster of rough wooden crosses in a field; dead German soldiers, still uncollected by the men of the Graves Commission.

Once again the oaks had come out to screen the scars of war along the road. The ditches were full of bright red flowers and on both sides the fields were swaying seas of yellow and green. Stolidly leather-shorted farmers plodded after their great lumbering red-brown oxen as they had done for centuries. The war had been over a year. The men who had fought it wanted to forget it; and now it seemed even nature was attempting to aid them in the task.

Nearly three months had passed since Schulze had slung an exhausted, drenched von Dodenburg over his shoulder, and scrambled up the rope ladder with the whistles and cries of alarm growing ever fainter behind them. For a month von Dodenburg had remained hidden in Schulze's brothel, presided over by the 'Belgian mare', as the ex-docker called the woman he lived with. At night he could hear the very men, who were searching for him by day, taking their sexual pleasure with Schulze's girls, with only a wall separating them from their quarry: the escaped SS officer, whose wanted poster was displayed everywhere throughout the American Zone of Occupation. With loving care Schulze and his 'Belgian mare' had tended him like a sick child until one day a beaming Schulze had entered his sick-room, ushering in a giggling, completely naked young whore.

Clicking his heels together as if he were still the Wotan's most senior NCO, he had snapped: 'Beg permission to offer you your lunch, sir!'

Von Dodenburg had looked from his broad grinning face to that of the giggling whore in bewilderment: 'What do you mean, er . . . Emile?'

Schulze had indicated the girl. 'You're cured, sir. I thought you might like this – to celebrate. Better than all that Belgian mare's soups. And she's new, sir. None of our noble American occupiers have had their big paws on her, have they, my little cheetah?'

Thereafter von Dodenburg's recovery from his suicide attempt and life in prison had progressed rapidly. He had grown stronger. His skinny frame had started to fill out – thanks to Schulze's mighty efforts on the thriving black market. Slowly he had begun to become restless, wandering around the house nervously when no 'guests' were present, until one day Schulze had cornered him and said, with all the realism of his newly acquired businessman's status: 'Sir, what are we going to do with you?'

'What do you mean, Emile?'

'Well, sir, as I see it, you can't stay here much longer. I mean there's a lot of lads in the old Wotan who would have given their right arm to have been able to spend the rest of their lives in a whorehouse. It would have been their idea of paradise.'

'But they are long dead,' von Dodenburg had reminded him softly.

'As I see it, sir, there are two possibilities. I provide you with a new identity and you start up something or other here in Germany. It's no problem to obtain papers these days.' He made a counting movement with his thumb and forefinger, 'Or,' he had hesitated momentarily. 'We set you off down the B-B line.'

'You mean?'

Schulze had nodded slowly. 'Yes, sir, you leave Germany –

and remember, sir, it means leaving for good. There is no way back, once you've gone.'

For what had seemed a long time von Dodenburg had considered the two alternatives, then not trusting himself to speak, he had traced two letters in the air with his forefinger. They had been 'B-B'.

Thus one month later they were now heading for the frontier, where on the Austrian side a professional smuggler was waiting to take him through the little country and on in to Italy, where another member of the Odessa[1] organization would convey him to a port, whence he would ship out for South America and a new life.

At midday, Schulze called a halt. They were at the base of the mountains and their orders were to cross the frontier just after dusk, the time when any curious frontier guard, surveying the area through his binoculars, would have difficulty picking them out in the growing shadows. Gratefully they sank down in the shade of a rusting Royal Tiger, metallic holes skewered along the length of its flank indicating how it had met its end a year or more before. Schulze handed von Dodenburg a packet of salami sandwiches prepared lovingly by the 'Belgian mare'. But von Dodenburg was not hungry. The knowledge that soon he would be leaving his country for good put him in a strangely reflective mood. Sipping at his flask of cold tea, he stared up at the monstrous tank, while Schulze champed on his food steadily at his side. There was no sound save the lazy hum of the bees in the red flowers of the dried-up ditches.

Idly he wandered around the back of the tank and rubbed the dust away from its fading divisional sign to reveal the springing greyhound of the 116th Panzer Division. 'The Greyhounds,' he announced. 'Von Schwerin's Division – they were with us at Aachen[2].'

Schulze nodded. 'A long time ago, sir,' he said, his mouth full of sausage and bread.

'Yes, a long time ago,' the handsome former Colonel agreed

[1] The 'Spider' organization was renamed 'Odessa' in early 1946. (*Transl.*)

[2] See *The Devil's Shield* for further details. (*Transl.*)

slowly. 'A bad time, yet somehow good – a sense of purpose, of doing something important. Remember all those young lads – those wet tails, you used to call them – how enthusiastic they were. Schulze?' His face lightened with sudden enthusiasm.

Schulze paused in the middle of a bite, the sweat running down his broad red face. 'Shall I tell you something, sir,' he said, pointing his sandwich at the man standing in front of him. 'I had my fun in the war – the girls, the larks, the booze and all the rest of it. But I paid my price in blood and misery. Life was so damn cheap then. Remember Sergeant Gierig just before the Ardennes? On the fifteenth, he said to me that if he bought it, I could have his leather coat. So what happens as soon as he copped one? I says "where's 'is shitty jacket?" We were all like that, sir, then. Heartless. Our lives weren't worth much more than that heap of cowshit over there in the field.' He finished the rest of his sandwich in one gulp. 'We lost the war, sir. It's all over now.' He looked intently at his former CO standing silently in the shadow cast by the tank. 'And in a way I'm glad we lost it.'

For what seemed a long time they faced each other thus, frozen into sudden inactivity, while within them that emotional change took place, which would destroy the relationship born of five years of war – that feeling of closeness, comradeship, utter dependence on one another, the sense of heart-warming liking for each other. Von Dodenburg shook his head, blinking in the sun like a man waking up from a deep sleep. The past was dead and the man squatting on his haunches in the dust was a stranger to him. Wordlessly he turned and started walking towards the mountain. After a moment Schulze followed.

* * *

Von Dodenburg kicked the little stone which marked the border. Down below the first of the night shadows was beginning to slide into the broad valley. In the sudden silence, he could hear the faint melodic sound of cowbells, as some farmer drove his animals down from the mountain pastures back to his farm. The Odessa guide would be waiting now on the other side of the grassy peak.

'Well, Schulze, this is the end of a long road.' He hesitated and made a last attempt. 'Don't you want to come with me after all, you big rogue?'

Schulze shook his big head. 'No sir, I don't want to come with you.' He stuck out his hand.

For a moment, von Dodenburg did not take it. He indicated the darkening valley. 'That down there, Schulze – that corrupt new conquered Germany is not worth dying for. You know that, don't you!'

Schulze shrugged, avoiding looking his former CO in the eyes. 'You might be right, sir . . . But one day there might be a Germany down there, worth living for.'

Von Dodenburg's face hardened. In stony silence, he took Schulze's outstretched hand and pressed it. But without warmth. Silently he swung round and began to climb the last few metres to the peak and the waiting guide. Momentarily he paused there, his shoulders bent, as if in defeat, but he did not look back. An instant later, Colonel Kuno von Dodenburg, the last commander of SS Battle Group Wotan, vanished for good.

'*Rome, Sat* (*dpa*). Yesterday, Nazi war criminal Kuno von Dodenburg passed away peacefully in his sleep in the capital's German Hospital. Reported cause of death was old war wounds. Von Dodenburg was in his early thirties. A ruthless, heartless, one hundred per cent National Socialist, von Dodenburg, the Armed SS's youngest colonel, commanded the infamous SS Thor Regiment during the war. Accused of complicity in war crimes, von Dodenburg escaped from the ex-U.S. Zone of Occupation with the aid of "friends in high places", according to Nazi-Hunter Number One, Simon Wiesenthal.

Asked to comment today, Wiesenthal stated from his office in Vienna, that Chancellor Adenauer "cannot continue to cover up for such wanted men – the Federal Republic must learn to clean out its own stables".

Kuno von Dodenburg left no known family. He will be buried in a pauper's grave in the Italian capital.'

News report in the West German magazine *Stern,* August 1952.